Chasing Bailey

A Lake Harriet Novel

Chasing Bailey
A Lake Harriet Novel

Copyright 2019 © Deanna Lynn Sletten

13: 978-1-941212-46-2
ISBN – 10: 1-941212-46-8

Cover Designer: Deborah Bradseth of Tugboat Design
Editor: Samantha Stroh Bailey of Perfect Pen Communications

Novels by Deanna Lynn Sletten

The Women of Great Heron Lake

Miss Etta

Night Music

One Wrong Turn

Finding Libbie

Maggie's Turn

As the Snow Fell

Walking Sam

Destination Wedding

Summer of the Loon

Sara's Promise

Memories

Widow, Virgin, Whore

Kiss a Cowboy

A Kiss for Colt

Kissing Carly

Outlaw Heroes

Chasing Bailey

A Lake Harriet Novel

DEANNA LYNN SLETTEN

Chapter One

Lisa Evans stepped up on her front porch as she juggled her two-year-old daughter, Abby, in one arm and a heavy bag in the other. She clumsily unlocked the front door, stepped inside the refreshing coolness of the living room, and set Abby down while also dropping the awkward bag to the floor. The bag tipped, spilling out Abby's toys, extra clothes, diapers, and snacks—all the items she needed for a full day at day care. At the same time, Abby ran down the hallway toward the back of the house hollering, "Baywee" in her little girl voice.

Lisa sighed. Another day completed.

She knelt, shoved all the items back into the bag, and turned to set it in the entryway closet. As she did, she caught sight of herself in the mirror. Her long blond hair was falling out of its ponytail and her scrub shirt printed with playful kittens had a big red stain on it. Thankfully, it wasn't blood like all the kids at school had thought when they'd stared at her with frightened faces. It was juice that had spilled as she'd poured some into Abby's cup at lunchtime. She was thankful that Abby's day care was next door to the school so she could eat lunch with her every day. But the stain was just another mishap that Lisa hadn't planned for.

Lisa walked across the room and dropped onto the sofa. She could still hear Abby pattering around the back of the house, calling out for Bailey. Lisa still had to make dinner, feed the dog, give Abby her bath, and put the little girl to bed. Then tomorrow it would start all over again. Only two weeks into being a working single mother and Lisa was already drained.

Abby came back into the living room and ran toward her mother. "No Baywee!" she cried, her tiny rosebud mouth drooping into a frown.

Lisa couldn't help but smile at the toddler's expression. Her round, little face and button nose were framed in silky auburn waves and her big green eyes were what drew the most attention from everyone who saw her. Normally, Abby was a sunny, happy child, but her favorite part of the day was coming home to her fluffy Border Collie. Not having him come running to her as they entered the house had obviously been a disappointment.

Then it hit Lisa. Bailey hadn't come running with excitement to see them. "Crap!" She scooped up her daughter and headed to the back door that led to their fenced-in backyard. "I'm sure he's here somewhere," she said, trying to convince herself more than trying to comfort Abby. She stared out the back door into the yard. Bailey had a doggie door that allowed him to go in and out as needed. But the yard was empty. No dog. Then, Lisa saw the hole.

"Crap!" she said again. Bailey had dug another escape route under their chain link fence.

"Cap!" Abby repeated.

Lisa grimaced. "Abigail Evans. Don't copy Mommy."

Abby grinned. "Cap!"

"Oh boy," Lisa said under her breath. She hurried toward the front of the house again with the intention of putting Abby in her wagon and walking the neighborhood in search of Bailey. But as she entered the living room, there was a pounding on the door. She almost said "crap" again but refrained. She was almost certain she knew who was there.

Setting Abby down on the floor, she went to answer. Sure enough, there stood the hermit from across the street holding her runaway dog by the collar and glowering at her.

"Baywee!" Abby yelled, arms wide open. Bailey pulled away from the man and ran to Abby. She wrapped her arms around her furry friend.

"I'm so sorry," Lisa said quickly to the man standing in front of her. His expression didn't soften in the least.

"He was digging in my yard again," he said. "What is it about *my* yard that he comes over there to dig? Why can't he run off to someone else's yard? This is the third time this month!"

The hermit looked really angry this time. The crease between his brows was deeper than normal. Of course, Lisa had never seen him do anything but scowl, but this was the worst one yet.

"I'm really sorry. I don't know why he's running to your yard either. He keeps digging a hole under the fence and I can't seem to stop him," Lisa said, which was true. Since she'd started working full time as a grade school nurse, Bailey had begun digging under the fence. Each time Lisa filled in the holes and placed large rocks over the area, he'd find a new spot to dig. She was at her wits' end trying to figure out how to solve the problem.

"Yeah. So you've said before," the man grumbled. He turned around and headed down the porch steps. "People who can't look after pets shouldn't have them," he said. It was more of a mumble but loud enough for her to hear.

Lisa's shoulders sagged as she shut the door. She already felt bad enough leaving the dog home alone all day. It didn't help to be told she was a bad pet parent too.

She turned and there sat Abby and Bailey, side-by-side, both smiling up at her. The sight of them warmed her heart, reminding her why she'd kept the unwanted dog in the first place. When her ex-husband, Andrew, had gifted the black and white puppy to Abby last May, Lisa had adamantly said no. There was no way she could care for a toddler and a puppy all by herself.

"All little kids need a puppy in their lives," he'd told her. And after only minutes, it was obvious that she couldn't make him return the dog. Abby fell in love and she and Bailey were best pals from that moment on. But now that he was a gangly five-month-old dog and Lisa was working, Bailey had become more of a nuisance than a playmate. Still, Lisa didn't have the heart to take Abby's dog away from her.

"Why can't you be more like Sam?" Lisa said, shaking her finger at the dog. "He never tries to run away. Sam, short for Samantha, was the beautiful, well-behaved golden retriever next door owned by Kristen and Ryan. Of course, she was also nine years old and well-trained, and poor Bailey hadn't had the benefit of training yet. Lisa felt lucky he was house-broken.

Bailey cocked his head and stared at her with that silly doggie grin. Lisa sighed. It was difficult being angry at Bailey.

"I know. I know. It's my fault you're not trained." She scooped Abby up as the little girl giggled with glee and headed toward the kitchen. Bailey followed, tail wagging. "Come on, you two. Let's eat dinner."

* * *

Avery McKinnon grumbled all the way across the street to his house. "Stupid dog. Why can't he just leave me alone?" He strode around the side of his two-bedroom bungalow and grabbed the shovel that stood against the back of the garage. Coming back out front, he began shoveling the loose dirt off the grass and back into the hole Bailey had dug.

"Annoying neighbors and their dumb dogs," he complained, growing more irritated with each shovelful of dirt. A car door slammed, making him turn to see who it was. The woman who lived next door to the annoying woman with the runaway dog was getting out of her car and lifting a toddler out of the back seat. She looked up, saw him staring, and waved. Avery quickly went back to his shoveling. He didn't know her name and didn't want to. He didn't have time for these bothersome people who had neighborhood parties and barbecues. When he'd moved here a year ago, he'd told the real estate woman that he wanted to live in a quiet neighborhood. No sooner had he moved in than neighbors were knocking on his door, welcoming him. He didn't want to be welcomed. He just wanted to be left alone.

After he'd shoveled and patted down the dirt, he returned the shovel to its place and went inside his house through the back door. Walking in the kitchen, he stopped at the refrigerator and stared inside it. There wasn't much there. He grabbed a cola and shut the door. It looked like tonight would be another pizza night.

As he passed his bedroom on the way to his office, Avery saw his reflection in the dresser mirror. Ugh! He looked awful. His hair was shaggy, and he hadn't shaved in several days. He glanced down at the flannel shirt he wore over his t-shirt and frowned. What was that stain? Yesterday's pizza? The stain brought to mind the woman across the street. He was sure he'd scared the daylights out of her with how he looked when he'd dragged her dog over there. Her blue eyes had been wide, and she'd talked in that nervous, high-pitched way women spoke when they were uncomfortable. And talk about stains. What the hell was that red splotch on that silly kitten shirt she was wearing? Did she perform surgery on someone? She'd looked a mess.

A quick stab of remorse hit Avery. No, the woman hadn't really looked a mess. She'd looked frazzled and tired. She'd probably worked all day and had just gotten home and still had the little girl to take care of all evening. And then there he was, right in her face, complaining about that dog. That sneaky, hole-digging dog that pulled a Houdini and escaped the backyard despite the chain link fence.

"Stop feeling sorry for that woman," he told himself as he entered the front bedroom that he used as an office. "She should find a way to keep that dog in her own yard."

He sat at his desk where he'd left his laptop open, the Word file staring back at him. "Now, where was I?" He scowled at the page, trying to remember his train of thought before he'd glanced out the window and had seen the dog digging. Running his fingers though his thick, dark hair, he studied the words he'd written half an hour ago.

"This story stinks!" he declared to the empty room. How on earth was he supposed to write a romance when he was still so angry over that crazy dog?

Taking a deep breath to clear his mind, he let his fingers start typing. *Big, blue eyes filled with tears as she gazed up at him. Her long, blond hair had come loose from its ponytail, and her shirt had some unknown stain on it, yet he hardly noticed. All he saw were those full, pink lips on that perfect face and he wanted to take her in his arms and kiss her.*

Avery stopped typing and glared at the words on the page. "What the hell is that?" He quickly backspaced through the paragraph, stood, and headed for the front door. He needed to take a long walk and get some fresh air. Maybe then he could sit down with a clear head and get back to work. The last thing he wanted to think about was some blond-haired woman with big blue eyes and pink lips. In fact, the last thing he needed in his life was any woman with any color of eyes or lips. He'd already had a woman in his life and been burned once. He didn't need to be burned again.

Slamming the front door, he stalked down the sidewalk with his hands in his pockets and his head down. He didn't want to see any neighbors or smile and wave to them. He just wanted to take his walk in peace.

Chapter Two

Before rushing out the door the next day, Lisa took a moment to stare at the doggie door in the back hallway. Last night, she'd filled the new hole Bailey had dug and covered it with large rocks and stones. But she knew Bailey would find a new spot to dig, and she didn't think it was safe to let him be outside while she was at work. Yet, she also feared he'd have an accident on the floor if he was left inside all day, and that could trigger a regression in his house breaking. Lisa sighed and made a quick decision to lock the doggie door. She might regret it, but at least Bailey would be safely indoors.

She quickly picked up Abby, her day care bag, and her purse and rushed out the kitchen door to her car parked in the driveway. As she carefully buckled her daughter into the car seat, she glanced over at the light blue, white shuttered bungalow where the angry hermit lived. The house was quiet and there was no movement or lights on inside to show that he was also getting ready for work. She wondered what he did for a living that allowed him so much time at home. "And so much time to judge me," she mumbled to herself.

"Cap!" Abby said gleefully.

Lisa eyed her daughter. "I didn't say that, you little monkey."

But she supposed her tone had triggered the little girl's memory.

Abby grinned at her and Lisa kissed her cheek. It was hard being mad at a sweet face like hers.

Later, at work, Lisa felt like she was going in ten different directions at once. Children came in with fevers and sniffles as harried parents arrived to pick them up. There were medications to distribute to children throughout the day and cuts and scrapes to fix with antiseptic and Band-Aids. The children didn't come and go in an orderly fashion as Lisa had been used to when she'd worked at a clinic before Abby was born. There had been appointments then; whereas now, it was chaos all the time as if she had a revolving door. She'd always believed being a school nurse would be easy compared to her old job. Boy, had she been wrong. As the day neared its end, she was thankful it was Friday and she'd have two days to recuperate before it all started again on Monday.

Upon arriving home later that afternoon, after Lisa picked up a bag of food from a burger place—chicken nuggets for Abby—and feeling guilty about buying her daughter fast food, Bailey rushed to meet them at the front door.

"At least you didn't run away," Lisa said, relieved she hadn't failed at that today. She set Abby down on the floor near the dog and headed into the kitchen. Immediately, she stepped into a huge puddle.

"Oh, Bailey." She sighed. Bailey had the good grace to look ashamed for having wet the floor. Lisa felt bad. It wasn't the dog's fault; it was hers. No dog should have to wait hours to go to the bathroom, especially a young one.

"It's okay, boy," she said, ushering the dog out to the backyard where he immediately did his business again. She returned to the kitchen and wiped up the mess.

Later, after they'd eaten, Lisa walked out into the yard to assess the fence issue. Abby had toddled out with her and was now rolling a huge ball around the grass while Bailey circled her. Lisa grinned at the sight. The first time she'd seen Bailey run circles around Abby, she'd thought the dog was playing. Then she'd realized that because Bailey was a herding dog, he was doing what came naturally to him. Bailey was just keeping tabs on his little friend to make sure she was safe.

Lisa studied the fence line as they played. The fence ran from the back of the house to the garage on the right side, then along the back property and up the other side where it stopped at the back of the house. The back fencing was taller—six feet—with green weave running through it for privacy. The side fencing was shorter with no weave. There were bushes every few feet inside the fence along the left side, and nothing along the inside fencing on the right that ran along their driveway to the garage. That was the section of fence where Bailey had done all of his digging.

Lisa wasn't sure what she should do to stop him. She'd put large rocks on the spots he'd dug, but there were plenty of open spaces. She really couldn't afford to place decorative rocks all along there. Nor did she want to do what her ex-husband had suggested—place an invisible fence around the yard that would shock Bailey every time he drew near it. Not only was an invisible fence expensive, she hated the thought of training a dog with a shock collar. Lisa sighed. On her one income and the limited amount of child support Andrew paid, she could hardly afford to do anything to the yard.

"Hi, Lisa. What are you pondering?"

Lisa looked up and saw Kristen coming through the hole in the hedges between their driveways and stopping next to her fence. She had her little blond, blue-eyed toddler, Marie, in one arm and was holding a jar of soup in the other.

"Hi, Kristen," she greeted with a smile. "Come on in and join us." She opened the gate latch and let Kristen through. Immediately, little Marie wanted down so she could run over to Abby. They were only four months apart in age and had been playing together almost since birth. The two little girls hugged then started running in circles, falling and laughing before running and falling again in some sort of made-up game. The women laughed along as they watched the girls while Bailey circled them.

"I brought you a fresh jar of chicken noodle soup," Kristen said, handing the old-fashioned Ball jar to Lisa.

Lisa brightened. "Thanks! I love your soup, and so does Abby. It's a lifesaver after a long day at work."

"I'm glad you enjoy it," Kristen said. "How's your new job?"

Lisa's shoulders sagged. "I'm thankful I have it and the hours are perfect, but to tell the truth, I'm beat. I never realized how hard it was to work all day and come home to a toddler. I guess I was spoiled before."

Kristen nodded. "I feel lucky I'm home full-time these days. Being an oncology nurse was draining, but I did love it. I'm sure I'll go back to work once the kids are older, but for now, this is all I can take."

Lisa's brows rose. "Kids?"

Kristen grinned. "Yeah. I just found out I'm three months pregnant."

"That's wonderful!" Lisa squealed, hugging her friend. "Congratulations!"

"Thanks," Kristen said. "Ryan is excited too. You're the first person I've told."

"I feel special," Lisa said with a laugh. "You're going to be a very busy woman in a few months."

Kristen nodded. "Yeah. It'll be strange to have two children, but I'm up for the challenge."

Lisa knew Kristen was more than up for the challenge. Ever since she'd moved into the neighborhood, when she and Andrew had bought the house from Kristen, she'd realized how amazing Kristen was. Kristen was not only a great mother, but she also cared about her neighbors and friends and always thought of others. She'd babysat for Lisa many times, expecting nothing in return, and had even been a shoulder to cry on when Andrew had left her last January. She was a true friend.

"What were you staring at when I interrupted you?" Kristen asked.

"Oh, Bailey escaped the yard again yesterday and of course he ran right for the hermit's house. So I made him stay inside all day and the poor boy had an accident on the floor. I'm trying to figure out how to stop him from digging under the fence."

Kristen studied the fence line. "So that's why you've been piling rocks near the fence."

Lisa nodded. "I don't know what else to do. I can't afford to have anything professionally done."

Kristen placed her hands on her hips. "Is Andrew still fighting you for joint custody?"

"Yes, he is. I honestly don't know why he wants to be an equal custodial parent, other than the child support would be set lower. He doesn't actually want Abby living with him full-time. It makes no sense. I think he's just being mean about the whole thing. Luckily, my attorney is working pro bono but I have to be extra careful with my money right now in case Andrew wins. That'll mean less money for me and Abby to live on."

Kristen shook her head in disgust. "Men! But don't worry.

We'll think of something to help you. We can't have that grouchy old hermit coming over here complaining."

Lisa smiled. "We?"

"Of course. It's the weekend. There must be something the neighborhood can do to help you. Leave it to me. We'll come up with something."

* * *

By Sunday, Kristen had organized the entire neighborhood. Soon, a parade of wheelbarrows carrying rocks of all shapes and sizes began making their way to Lisa's house. Ryan, James, and the new neighbor, Matthew Carpenter—who rented the house on the other side of Lisa with his wife, Kaylee, and their one-year-old son, Theodore—were in charge of placing the rocks along the inside of the fence. Lisa supplied the burgers for their cookout and the raw veggies while Kristen brought chips and buns. Mallory brought a tub of ice that held juice boxes, cola, and beer for the grown-ups. Kaylee brought hot dogs and chicken strips for the kids and Debbie, the owner of Deb's Bridal Shop, who lived on the other side of the Carpenters, brought cake for dessert. Everyone supplied the rocks from their yard-scast off boulders and rocks picked up as the owners had mowed or dug up gardens.

Along with their children, everyone had brought their dogs. Sam was there, seemingly watching over the other dogs to make sure they behaved. Brewster, James' bulldog, Bailey, and Deb's little puffball of a dog, Chloe, all ran around the yard with the children. They had set up a couple of blow-up pools without water to use as playpens and filled them with toys. It was a happy group of neighbors enjoying a beautiful fall afternoon.

Lisa watched as the men lined the bigger rocks about two feet in from the fence then used the smaller rocks to fill in. It wasn't fancy, but it should work. She was thankful for her neighbors who cared enough to help her. She didn't know too many neighborhoods these days like hers.

As she started up the grill and the women brought out the plates of food to place on it, she smiled. At least now she wouldn't have to worry about Bailey digging under the fence. And that meant no more hermit from across the street.

* * *

Avery was sitting at his desk, typing nonstop all Sunday morning, finally focused on his novel. It was due to his editor in thirty days and he'd only just started it. But that wasn't anything new. He'd written a book in a month before. He could do it again—as long as there weren't any interruptions.

Early afternoon, he stopped typing as hunger pains gripped him. As he stood to go into the kitchen, he glanced out the window that faced the street. A parade of wheelbarrows filled with rocks were being pushed down the street toward that pesky woman's house.

"What the hell?"

He watched, mesmerized, as neighbors came and went from her house. A few women were bringing grocery bags filled, he assumed, with food. People were milling around her yard and driveway. But most of the activity seemed to be going on in her backyard.

Avery wrinkled his nose. "Another one of those annoying neighborhood barbeques," he grumbled. "But what's up with the rocks?" He strode into his kitchen and grabbed a beer, bread, and lunchmeat out of his fridge. The kitchen had been remodeled before he bought the bungalow, so it was open to the living room with an island as a divider. The new cabinets were white and topped with black granite countertops. More than likely chosen by a woman, he'd thought when he'd first looked at the house. Just like the exterior paint. Light blue with white shutters. Definitely chosen by a woman. Men generally chose darker colors. But despite all that, it had been the right price for that moment, and he'd been in desperate need of a place to live, so he'd purchased it.

As he made his sandwich, he couldn't help but see the stream of people coming and going. He looked at the pile of mail on the counter. Usually someone placed a cutesy flyer in everyone's mailbox announcing these neighborhood events. He always balled them up and threw them in the trash. But as he searched through his mail, he didn't see one.

"I wouldn't have gone anyway," he muttered, returning to his sandwich.

Still, it seemed rather impolite for them not to at least invite him.

He found an almost empty bag of chips in the cupboard and placed a handful on his sandwich plate, then took it and his beer to his desk. He didn't care that the whole neighborhood was having a party without him. He had work to do. After taking a bite of his food and a swig of beer, he returned his attention to the manuscript.

She smiled at him from across the tiny living room, her blue eyes dark with passion. Her long hair fell around her bare shoulders, soft and silky in the flickering candlelight. He'd waited a long time for this moment, the moment when he'd finally be able to cross the space between them and hold her in his arms. As he strode across the space that separated them, he suddenly tripped over the rambunctious dog running right under his feet.

"What?" Avery looked at the paragraph he'd typed. "There's no dog in my book. And the main character has dark hair, not blond. Sheesh!" Quickly, he backspaced through the unwanted paragraph. What was wrong with him? Every time he sat down to write, his mind was on that woman across the street with the cute kid and runaway dog. She was driving him crazy!

"In more ways than one," he admitted softly to himself. He turned in his seat and began scarfing down his lunch between swigs of beer. He was mad at himself for waiting so long to finish this novel. He was angry at that annoying dog and the woman who let it wander the streets. But most of all, he was upset with himself for finding her attractive, despite everything. And worst yet, she was married, wasn't she? He pondered that a moment, trying to picture who her husband was. Nothing came to mind.

"Ugh! I need a life," he said, and polished off the rest of his food. Sitting back in his chair, he looked around his office: a tiny, square room with nothing personal in it except his computer and a few boxes that held copies of his past novels. There were shelves on the wall, but after a year of living here, he hadn't bothered to put anything on them. That was true of the whole house. Other than a few pieces of scattered furniture, he'd hardly emptied any of the boxes he'd packed with his belongings.

At thirty-six years old, he felt like he was starting his life all over again.

He'd had a life once. His office used to be large and beautiful, with built-in glass cases for his books and awards, and a large picture window with a lake view. His house had sat on two lush acres with big trees and there'd been a great path around the lake where he could walk with his dog in silence and think about his next book. He'd also had a wife, a dreamy woman with long, black hair and luscious lips who'd thought he was amazing. They'd traveled together, hiked in exotic locations, skied in Aspen, and spent a week every winter at a gorgeous resort in the Bahamas. Their life had been perfect.

Until she'd found a new guy and thrown Avery out. She'd taken everything. The house, half of the money, and even the dog. The dog for Pete's sake! And then he'd ended up here.

Avery sighed.

He turned back to his computer and reread a few paragraphs to jump-start his writing again. The heroine resembled his ex-wife too much. Maybe that was why he had trouble remembering how she looked. She was one woman he didn't want to think about. But changing the woman's appearance wouldn't help either. It would only remind him of the woman across the street.

"Maybe she should be a redhead," he mumbled.

Looking up, he saw one of the neighborhood women walking through the tall hedge between her house and the pesky woman's house—he really should learn her name—and go inside. She returned a minute later with a bottle of ketchup and headed for the backyard.

Yep. They were grilling. "Good for them," he said sarcastically. He thought about the hole in the tall hedge between their houses. Neighbors must have been going between houses for years for that to be there. He used to have neighbors he liked. Couples who'd drop by for a drink sometimes in the evenings or a group of them would go out for a burger and beer. He and his wife entertained friends quite a bit. But that all ended the day she won the house, the dog, and even the neighbors in the divorce settlement.

No longer in the mood for writing, Avery closed his laptop

and stood, stretching his muscles. He also missed his home gym where he'd run on his treadmill or use his Bowflex while watching the sixty-inch flat-screen television. He was getting badly out of shape.

Grabbing a clean flannel shirt to pull on over his T-shirt, he headed outside to take a walk. He figured he'd head to Lake Harriet and follow the path around it. The lake would be peaceful this time of year with the leaves just beginning to turn their fall colors. He could get his mind off his ex-wife, his book, and most of all, the woman across the street.

Chapter Three

Late Tuesday afternoon, Avery decided it was time to give himself a break. For three glorious days, he'd been writing non-stop and the book—while still a little shaky in places—was going along fairly well. It had helped to change the heroine, but the biggest help was not having that rogue dog digging up his yard.

For the first time in a long while, he felt good. He decided he'd get out of the house and drive downtown to his favorite place to eat a delicious burger and fries. He changed into a nice shirt and a pair of jeans and slipped on his favorite pair of black western boots. Then he jumped into his black SUV—the only thing he'd actually been allowed to keep after the divorce—and drove into downtown Minneapolis.

Twenty minutes later, he found a parking space a block away from the bar and walked the rest of the way. When he saw the sign next to the door, he smiled. Gallagher's Irish Pub. He hadn't eaten here in over a year and felt joy just looking at it.

Walking inside, he saw the place was only a quarter full since it was still too early for the dinner crowd. He found a table against the back wall and sat on the high stool. After a moment, a dark-haired man with a white rag slung over his shoulder came to the table with a menu.

"Hello there," the man said. "What can I get you to drink?"

Avery assumed he was the bartender. He'd never seen him in here before. Usually a friendly redheaded woman waited on the tables. "Any local beer you have on tap," Avery told him. "I like to try new ones."

The man smiled. "Great. I'll be back in a sec."

Avery placed the paperback he'd brought on the table. He figured he could sit back and read while he enjoyed his meal. He loved reading, mostly crime novels, thrillers, or suspense, or anything Stephen King wrote, but he hadn't had a lot of downtime in a while. He realized that it was humorous that he read novels so different from the romance ones that he wrote. The first novel he'd ever written was a suspense similar to what James Patterson wrote, except no one thought he was an up-and-coming James Patterson, especially the agents he'd sent it to. Next, he'd tried a softer-style suspense that featured a female lead character. That time, an agent saw potential, but not for suspense. "Have you ever thought of writing romance?" the agent had asked him.

"Like Danielle Steel?" he'd asked, skeptically.

"Well, more like Nicholas Sparks," the agent had said. "You have a writing style that I think would be perfect for that genre. And there's good money in romance."

Avery hadn't been convinced, but he figured it couldn't hurt. At first, it hadn't been easy, but then, when he'd met Melissa and fallen completely in love, it was as if the romance faucet had been turned on. Writing love stories that were deep and heartfelt seemed to come easily to him.

But that was then. Now—it was difficult to find any good in love and romance after being broken.

"Here's your beer," the man said, bringing him a tall mug. "Hope you like it. It's a new one we're trying from a local brewer."

Avery nodded. He took a sip. It was a bit heavy, but good. "Not too bad," he said. He ordered his burger and fries, but before the man turned to leave, Avery noticed a brown blob with four legs coming up behind the bartender.

"What is that?" Avery asked, pointing to the creature.

The man looked down, then laughed. "That's Brewster, my dog. He's our bar mascot."

Avery stared at the pug-nosed dog with wrinkles all over it. "A bulldog?"

"Yep."

"I've never seen him in here before," Avery said.

"I usually take him home at night. He just hangs around here with me during the day."

Avery squinted. Something about the dog seemed familiar. "I'd swear I've seen that dog in my neighborhood. But I suppose they all look the same."

"Don't tell Brewster that. He thinks he's one of a kind," the man said with a grin. "Where do you live?" When Avery told him the street, the man nodded. "Yep. It's Brewski you've seen. We must be neighbors." He held out his hand to shake. "James Gallagher."

"Avery McKinnon."

"Ah. A good Scottish name," James said.

"It is. So, you must be the owner?"

"I am," James said. "The place has been in the family for generations. A couple of years ago I came home and reopened the bar after my father passed." He stared at Avery. "You know, you do look familiar. I'm surprised we've never met. Our neighborhood is so friendly. Everyone knows everybody."

Avery nearly rolled his eyes. "Yeah. I've noticed. To be honest, I keep to myself."

James' eyes brightened as though a lightbulb had gone off in his head. "Oh. You're the hermit across the street," he said, then laughed.

"What?"

James suddenly looked contrite. "Sorry. I shouldn't have said that. You must be the guy who has to keep bringing Lisa's dog home. She's been upset about that."

Avery frowned. Upset about what? That the dog ran away or that he kept bringing him back? "Well, it is kind of annoying that it keeps digging holes in my yard," he grumbled.

James smiled. "I'm sure it is, and she feels terrible about it. I think we've solved the problem, though, so hopefully Bailey won't be in your yard again."

Avery wondered what they'd done to solve the problem, but he didn't want it to sound like he cared enough to ask. "That's good."

"I'll go put your order in. It's nice meeting you," James said. "Maybe I'll see you around the neighborhood."

"Yeah. Nice meeting you." Avery looked down and watched as Brewster followed James back to the bar. *Funny looking dog*, he thought. But watching Brewster follow his owner brought back memories of his own dog following him on walks around their yard and in the park. He missed Maddie—much more than he missed his ex, Melissa. Maddie was a beautiful five-year-old Irish Setter. He'd trained her himself and she'd been the perfect dog. For the life of him, he couldn't understand why Melissa had fought to keep her—except to hurt him. She'd been the one who wanted the divorce, so why punish him?

A young woman with short blond hair brought his food and another beer, and Avery dived into it. It was the perfect blend of juicy and greasy, just like bar food should be. They had the best fries here, too. Sitting back and savoring his food, he picked up his novel and began reading. This was the perfect ending to a great day. Even though he knew he'd be up late working on his book, he was enjoying himself right now.

And then his happy bubble popped. The very reason he hadn't been in Gallagher's for over a year walked into the pub holding hands with her new flame.

Avery couldn't help but stare at Melissa as she glided so effortlessly in her heels, her skirt short enough to tastefully show off her long, lean legs. Her red sweater fit her curves perfectly and her long, dark hair swung ever so slightly as she moved toward the middle of the room. She had one arm linked around her boyfriend's arm and she was smiling up at him as if he were the smartest man in the world.

Avery's face wrinkled up into a sneer. She used to look at him that way.

As Avery watched them settle in a booth across the room, he couldn't help but wonder what this guy Ross had that he didn't. He was younger than Avery—thirty-two years old like Melissa while Avery was four years older—but that couldn't have made much difference. He was tall with an athletic build, much like Avery was, or at least the way Avery had been before the divorce, but from there the comparison ended. Ross had sandy blond hair, blue eyes, and a ridiculous goatee. Avery hated goatees, but apparently, they didn't bother Melissa. He had money, too, but then, Avery used to have money before his wife took half of it. The part that infuriated Avery most, though, was that Ross Gunderson inherited all of his money instead of worked for it. Ross's father owned several large car dealerships across the Twin Cities and all Ross had to do was show up once in a while to get his paycheck. At least that was how it seemed to Avery. The guy drove a sports car, owned a house on a very prestigious lake outside of the cities, and even had access to his own private jet.

And Avery now lived in a bungalow in an older neighborhood. Well, at least he earned his money and wasn't given it. She could have the pretentious snob for all he cared.

Avery sighed. So why did it still bother him?

His appetite gone, Avery decided to leave the bar before Melissa saw him. The last thing he wanted was to be stuck trying to make nice small talk to her or Mr. Trust Fund.

He waved the waitress over and asked for his check. When she brought it, she glanced at his half-empty plate and asked, "Was there something wrong with your food?"

"No, no," he said hurriedly. "It was fine. I just realized I had to be somewhere." *Yeah, anywhere but here!* He dropped a couple of twenties on the table and headed for the door. He was almost past the bar when James called out, "See you around, Avery."

Avery stopped and turned toward James and immediately saw Melissa staring at him. Their eyes locked, and he felt like a deer caught in headlights. Finally, he broke his gaze, waved at James, and strode out the door.

* * *

Lisa's week was going well. Her neighbors coming together to help her on Sunday had really lifted her spirits. And since then, each day had run smoothly. She thought maybe it was because the stress of Bailey escaping the yard was finally gone. Or maybe she was getting the hang of being a working mom. Whatever it was, she was happy everything was going well.

Wednesday after school, Lisa picked Abby up from day care and they went grocery shopping before heading home. She kept

Abby placated in the cart with a small bag of animal crackers. As soon as they arrived home, Lisa planned on heating up the soup Kristen had given them and also the corn bread she'd bought at the store's bakery. Nothing was better than a warm piece of corn bread with melted butter on it. Her mouth watered at the thought of it.

Once home, she brought Abby inside and quickly began hauling in the groceries. Abby ran around inside the house, looking for Bailey, and since Lisa was busy, she didn't think twice about the dog not rushing in to greet the little girl. Bringing in the last of the bags, Lisa stopped and glanced around.

No Bailey.

"Crap!"

She quickly ran to the back door where Abby was standing, staring out at the empty yard.

"No Baywee," Abby said sadly.

Lisa scanned the yard, unable to believe the dog would have found an escape route. But then her eyes fell on it. Bailey had dug up the rocks and then a hole so he could slip under the fence.

"Cap?" Abby asked, looking up at her mother.

Lisa's shoulder's sagged. "Cap," she agreed. She scooped up the little girl and headed through the house. Maybe if she could find Bailey first, she'd be able to avoid a confrontation with the hermit. She stepped outside onto the covered front porch, then realized she'd forgotten her keys.

"Wait here one second," she told Abby. Lisa ran two steps into the house for her purse and two steps back to the front porch. As she looked up, two angry blue eyes glared back at her.

"What's wrong with you?" the hermit growled at her, his hand holding Bailey's collar. "Not only can't you control your dog, but then you leave your child on the front porch, alone. Are you crazy? If I were a creep, I could have grabbed her and been gone before you even knew she was missing!"

Lisa's mouth dropped open at his angry words. He wasn't just annoyed, he was fuming. "I was only gone for a moment," she tried to explain, but the hermit interrupted her.

"That's all it takes. A moment. Just a quick second alone on the porch and this sweet little girl could have been taken." He released Bailey and the dog ran up the steps to Abby. "You don't deserve to have a dog or a kid," the hermit said, looking her right in the eyes. Then he turned and stormed off across the street.

Lisa's mind spun as she tried to digest what he'd said. She fell in one of the chairs on the porch as she stared at her daughter, innocently hugging Bailey. She'd failed again, and this time, it was big. The hermit was right—she shouldn't have left Abby on the porch, not even for a split second. That was all it took for a child to be taken. She was a terrible mother. Devastated, she dropped her head in her hands and collapsed into tears.

"Lisa! Lisa! What's wrong? Are you okay?" Kristen ran up on the porch as quickly as she could while carrying little Marie. "Sweetie. Why are you crying? Did that guy from across the street do this?"

Lisa looked up at her friend as shame washed over her. Shame for her incredible lack of judgment for leaving Abby unattended on the porch, and shame that Kristin was seeing her cry over what that horrid man had said to her. The stress of the last few months engulfed her. Just when she'd thought she was doing okay, she'd failed miserably, and the tears wouldn't stop falling.

Kristen set Marie down next to Abby and Bailey then knelt beside Lisa. "What happened? Tell me what I can do."

Between sobs, Lisa explained how Bailey had escaped again, and how she'd thoughtlessly left Abby on the porch—for only a moment—but a moment too long. "I'm a terrible mother," she said as tears streamed down her face. "If anything happened to Abby, I'd just die."

Kristen rubbed her back, then went inside for tissues and handed them to Lisa. "You're not a terrible mother," she told her with certainty. "You're a wonderful mother doing the best you can. And that horrible man had no right yelling at you like that. I swear, I'm going over there right now to tell him what I think."

"What's going on?" Ryan came up on the porch, his face creased with concern. "I just pulled up and saw you both here." He turned to Kristen. "And who are you going to tell off?"

"That awful guy across the street. He's rude and unsociable and he's made Lisa cry. It's time someone told him off." She explained what the hermit had said to Lisa. "He had no right saying that to her," Kristen said when she'd finished.

Lisa had calmed down a little and was wiping her tears. "Please, don't make a fuss over it. Bailey did run over to his place again, after all. And I left Abby on the porch, unattended."

"But he can't call you a terrible mother," Kristen said, her voice rising. "I want to have a few words with him."

Ryan placed a hand on his wife's shoulder. "Honey. You can't just go over there and start yelling at the guy."

"Then you do it," Kristen said. "Tell him to lay off Lisa. Punch him if you have to."

Lisa panicked. She didn't want Ryan to get into a brawl because of her.

Ryan shook his head. "I'm not going to punch him," he told Kristen. "I'll go talk to him, though. You're right. He has no right talking to Lisa that way."

Kristen stared at Ryan a moment, then let out a sigh. "Fine. I'll stay here with Lisa. But don't be nice about it. Tell him in no uncertain terms that he has to straighten up or he can just move."

Ryan nodded. "I will. I'll go see what he has to say for himself."

Chapter Four

Avery sat in his house feeling like a jerk. He couldn't believe he'd just told that woman she shouldn't be allowed to raise a kid. It was a terrible thing to say. No, it was more than terrible, it was appalling. But in his defense, he'd been upset finding that stupid dog in his front yard again, digging a hole. And when he'd hauled the dog back to her house, there stood that cute little girl, all alone on the porch. For some unknown reason, that made him flip out.

And now he felt guilty as hell.

The look on the woman's face after he'd yelled at her was burned into his brain. She'd looked like she was going to faint. He'd left so quickly he hadn't looked back to make sure she was okay. He'd been afraid that if he turned around, he wouldn't have been able to leave. He felt so horrible, he knew he'd have run back and apologized over and over again. So he'd stuck to his resolve and gone home.

Cripes. What kind of creep had he become? In that moment, he truly hated himself.

A pounding on his front door made him jump. "Who in the world is that?" he said aloud. Avery looked out the peephole. One of the men from across the street was standing there, looking angry.

He's probably here to punch me out. With a sigh, Avery opened the door.

"What were you thinking, talking to Lisa like that?" the guy said, scowling at Avery.

Avery was unable to come up with a good answer. "Are you her husband?"

The man looked confused for a second. "No. I live next door to her. You upset Lisa with your cruel words and then it upset my wife. And man, you're lucky my wife didn't come over here because she was fuming."

Avery looked past the man and over at the pesky woman's— Lisa's—porch. It was empty now. He assumed this guy was married to that other woman who had the kid about the same age as Lisa's.

"You know, everyone is this neighborhood is nice. We all try to get along. We've invited you to our neighborhood events and you've never come to any of them. So we've all tried to leave you alone, since that's what you seem to want. Still, you have the nerve to yell at Lisa."

"Yeah, but her dog keeps coming over here and digging up my yard," Avery said, trying to defend himself. He knew as soon as the words left his mouth it was an inadequate excuse.

"So that gives you the right to call her a terrible mother? You don't know the first thing about Lisa. Because if you did, you'd know she's a kind and caring mother to Abby and a wonderful person."

Avery winced. The guy was right. He'd had no right to go as far as telling her she didn't deserve having a child. "Would you like to come in for a beer?" he asked. It looked like he'd totally thrown the guy off.

"What? A beer? Huh?"

"Maybe we can talk about this calmly over a beer. Or a soda, if you'd rather," Avery said.

"Oh. Yeah." The guy ran his hand through his hair and looked over his shoulder at Lisa's house. "Well, uh, sure. I'll have a beer," he said.

Avery moved aside and let him in. Then he walked across the living room to the kitchen and grabbed two bottles of beer from the fridge. The man had followed him to the island and was glancing around.

"By the way, I'm Avery," he said, handing the guy the beer.

"Ryan. Ryan Collier," the guy said.

They both stared at each other. Each took a sip of beer, then Ryan spoke again.

"I've never been in this house before. It was empty for a couple of years before you bought it. It looks nice."

"Thanks, but no credit goes to me. I haven't done a thing to it since I've moved in."

"You've lived here over a year, haven't you?" Ryan asked, eyeing the unopened boxes in the living room.

"Yeah. I guess I haven't really made myself at home yet."

Ryan nodded, as if he understood. "So, about Lisa."

Avery raised his hand up to stop him. "I get it. I was an idiot to her. To tell the truth, I was in here regretting what I'd said before you came over."

Ryan raised a brow. "Okay. Are you going to apologize to her?"

"Yeah. I was just trying to think of a way to make it up to her. I know she's trying to keep the dog out of my yard. For some reason, though, that dog keeps heading over here."

Ryan nodded. "Bailey's a good dog. Border Collies are

smart. He just needs some training, and unfortunately, Lisa is too swamped with work and raising Abby to take care of it. She's doing the best she can."

Avery motioned for them to sit on the leather sofa in the living room and Ryan did.

"Doesn't her husband help?" Avery asked. "I thought she was married."

Ryan studied him a moment before answering. "Actually, she and her husband split this past January. And no, he doesn't help much except taking Abby every other weekend. He's also the one who gave Abby the puppy for a present without Lisa's permission."

"Oh. I see." Avery was getting a clearer picture of the situation. "So, she wasn't prepared for a lively puppy."

"No, she wasn't." Ryan took another sip of beer. "You know, what Bailey really needs is a little exercise to wear off his energy every day. I've noticed that you take long walks. Did you ever think of asking Lisa if you could take Bailey along? He'd be less likely to dig if he had exercise."

"No, I guess that never occurred to me." Avery sat back and thought about it. Truth be told, he'd been too absorbed with being angry about everything in his life to ever think that she needed a little help. "I've gotten a little rusty when it comes to the nice neighbor thing."

"Well, it couldn't hurt to try. Who knows? Maybe you and Lisa could even be friends," Ryan said, a grin tugging at his lips.

Avery laughed. "Yeah. If she ever talks to me again."

Ryan finished his beer, then stood. "Thanks for the beer. I'm glad we were able to talk this out. To tell the truth, I really didn't want to fight anyone today." He chuckled.

"Me neither." Avery walked Ryan to the door. "I met another

neighbor the other night. James Gallagher. He seems like a nice guy."

Ryan nodded. "He is. And his wife is nice too. She owns a staging and design business. In fact, most of the people who live in this neighborhood are pretty great people, if you give them a chance."

"Point taken," Avery said. "You know, I'm not really that bad of a guy. It's just been a difficult year for me, and I guess I took out my anger on this neighborhood, and Lisa. I shouldn't have done that."

"I know where you're coming from. I had a few tough years too, before I met Kristen. Things do get better." He grinned. "Speaking of Kristen, it took a lot of convincing to keep her from coming over here and giving you an earful. Next time you may not be so lucky."

"Hmm. She's a tough one, huh?"

"She worked as a pediatric oncology nurse for years before staying home with our little girl. She's had to be tough to stay strong at her job. But she has a big heart and is loyal to her friends. She's pretty amazing."

"She sounds like she is. I promise I won't give her any more reasons to come here and straighten me out," Avery said.

"Great." Ryan waved and walked out the door.

As Avery watched him leave, he stared across the street to where Lisa lived. He wondered how he'd make it up to her. Closing the door, he had an idea.

* * *

An hour later, Avery stood at Lisa's door with a large pizza, a box of chicken strips, and a bottle of wine. He rang the bell and immediately heard the dog barking. A moment later, Lisa opened the door a little and stared at him. Her eyes were bloodshot, and her face was tear-streaked. He felt horrible. He'd been the one who'd made her cry.

"What do you want?" she asked, frowning at the boxes in his hand.

"I came over to apologize," he said quickly so she wouldn't slam the door in his face. He wouldn't have blamed her if she had, though. "I shouldn't have said what I did. It was cruel and certainly not true. It's obvious you're a good mother. I see you nearly every day carefully buckling your little girl in and out of her car seat and taking her for walks around the neighborhood in her little wagon. I've seen you hold her while talking to neighbors, giving her tiny kisses on her cheeks for no reason other than because you love her. I'm so sorry I said what I did."

Lisa's frown deepened. "You've been watching me?"

Avery realized how creepy that must have sounded. "No. I mean, yeah. I mean, not intentionally. My office is in the front bedroom and my desk faces the window. I see a lot that goes on in the neighborhood."

She continued to stare at him, as if gauging what he'd said. From behind her, he saw Abby sitting on the floor, rolling a ball for Bailey to retrieve. The dog would run after it and bring it back to her so she could roll it again. He smiled. "Your daughter is teaching your dog how to play fetch."

Lisa looked startled a moment, then turned and watched what he'd seen. Turning back, her expression had softened. "Yes, she is. She adores Bailey. They play together all the time."

The sweet look in Lisa's blue eyes when she spoke about her daughter made Avery's smile widen. "I'm Avery. Avery McKinnon. I'm sorry I never introduced myself before. It would have been the polite thing to do."

"I'm Lisa," she said, looking more comfortable. "And I accept your apology, if you really meant what you said."

"I do mean it," he said. He didn't know exactly what had made him soften toward her. Her smile? The way her eyes gleamed when she looked at her daughter? Whatever it was, his heart didn't feel as cold and shut off as it had over the past year. "Oh. I brought you pizza, and chicken strips for your daughter," he said, indicating the boxes in his hands. "I wasn't sure if after everything that happened, you'd had time to cook dinner."

Lisa's eyes moved to the bottle of wine.

"And the wine is part of the apology," he added.

Lisa opened the door a little wider and both Bailey and Abby glanced up at Avery. "Actually, we haven't eaten yet, unless you call crackers dinner." She took the boxes from him. "Thanks for thinking of this." She walked to the dining room table and placed the boxes there.

"It's the least I could do." He was still standing outside the door and holding the bottle of wine. He wasn't sure if he should stay or leave.

Lisa turned to him. "Would you like to join us?"

Avery smiled. He hadn't been expecting an invitation, but he realized he really wanted to stay. "Thank you. I would." He walked inside, closing the door behind him.

Chapter Five

Lisa sat across the table from the hermit—oops, Avery—eating a piece of pizza and sipping the wine he'd brought. She could hardly believe they were here together after all that had transpired earlier. The pizza was delicious, and of course Abby liked the chicken strips. Lisa had brought out some cut-up veggies, too, and salad that she'd prepared the day before. Abby was as comfortable with Avery being there as if he ate with them every night. And Bailey was, too.

Now that she'd had a closer look at Avery, and he wasn't glaring as he'd typically done, she realized that he wasn't bad looking. His dark hair was a bit long, as if he hadn't had it cut in a while, but it didn't look shaggy. And he was freshly shaven, which had surprised her too. He'd always had that scruffy look before. But what caught her off guard the most were his deep blue eyes trimmed in dark lashes. Despite his always being grouchy toward her, now she saw that his eyes looked kind, especially when he smiled.

"I wasn't expecting you to invite me in to eat, but I'm glad you did," he said. "It's nice eating with someone for a change instead of alone."

She nodded, not sure what to say. She figured hermits liked

to eat alone. "I hope Ryan didn't make you do this," she said. "I honestly didn't send him over to talk to you. Kristen, his wife, did."

"No. Ryan didn't tell me to do this. This was my idea. I felt terrible the second the words came out of my mouth, but I was too ornery to apologize then and there. Once I got home, I knew I'd gone too far. But I did have a nice talk with Ryan. He's a good guy."

"He is. And Kristen is great, too. This is a wonderful neighborhood. Everyone is always willing to lend a hand."

"So I've been told," Avery said. "I noticed there was a big neighborhood get-together at your place last Sunday."

Lisa thought a second then remembered. "Oh, yeah. That wasn't a planned thing. Everyone came over to help fix my yard so Bailey wouldn't dig a hole and escape again. I guess it didn't work as well as we'd thought."

Upon hearing the dog's name, Abby smiled wide and said, "Baywee!" Bailey responded by getting up from where he'd been lying and running over to sit beside Abby's highchair.

Avery laughed, a deep, warm chuckle. "She's adorable," he said, grinning at Abby. "Your puppy sure does love you."

"Baywee!" Abby said again, enjoying the attention.

"And she loves Bailey," Lisa said. She turned to Avery. "It's been frustrating having him run away, especially since he goes to your yard all the time. I'm at a loss what to do now."

Avery nodded. "I understand that now. Maybe I can take a look at your yard and see what else can be done. The most important thing is that Bailey doesn't get out and get hit by a car."

"I've worried about that too," Lisa said. It had been something she'd feared the most, even more than facing the hermit, uh,

Avery. If anything happened to Bailey, how would she explain it to Abby? "If you have any ideas for the yard, I'm open to them."

"I'd be happy to look," he offered.

Abby was finished eating so Lisa began clearing the table. She'd only had one glass of wine, but it had warmed her from the inside and helped to calm her nerves. Avery pitched in, and even lifted Abby out of her high chair after Lisa had wiped her little face.

Abby toddled after Avery into the kitchen, which meant that Bailey followed too. Avery wrapped up the leftover pizza and put it in the fridge while Lisa rinsed the dishes and placed them in the dishwasher. The whole time, Abby followed Avery around and watched him.

"It looks like you've made a new friend," Lisa said to Avery, indicating her daughter beside him.

"I could use a new friend." He smiled down at Abby, then lifted that smile up to Lisa. "Or, maybe two new friends."

Lisa felt an unexpected warmth rush up her neck and face. She couldn't believe she was blushing. But as she looked at Avery, she understood why. When he wasn't glowering, he was actually charming. That thought surprised her so much that she quickly changed the subject.

"So, what is it that you do that keeps you in the front bedroom working day and night?" she asked. As the words left her mouth, she realized how they sounded and a new blush rose into her cheeks. It didn't help that Avery grinned and raised his brows.

"Well," he said, drawing it out.

"You know what I meant," she said hurriedly.

He chuckled. "I'm a writer. I sit at my computer all day and spend most of my time staring out the window instead of writing."

This surprised her. "Really? I would never have guessed that."

"That I stare out the window or that I'm a writer?"

"That you're a writer," she said. "What do you write?"

She noticed he paused before answering, making her wonder if she was prying. "You don't have to answer that," she said quickly. "It's really none of my business."

"I don't mind answering, although people generally act weird when I tell them. I write novels."

"Novels. That's amazing. Anything I might have read?"

He chuckled. "That depends on what you read. Have you read any good romances lately?"

Her mouth involuntarily dropped open and it took a moment for her to realize she was gawking at him. She clamped her jaw shut.

"See what I mean?" he asked. "You're acting strange."

Lisa felt awful for the way she'd reacted. But it was really hard to believe that the man she'd thought of as the cranky hermit was sitting in his house writing romances. "I'm sorry. I didn't mean to react that way. But really? Romance? I didn't expect that at all."

He shrugged. "I know. I get that all the time. But there are men who write romance. It's not that odd."

She nodded. "I know. But it still surprises me." She frowned as she thought for a moment. "Wait. You said your name is Avery McKinnon?"

"Yep."

Lisa walked out into the living room with the whole parade of Avery, Abby, and Bailey following her. She headed for the built-in bookshelf beside the television. After studying it a moment, she pulled out a paperback and showed it to him. "This Avery McKinnon?"

Avery glanced at the book cover. "Guilty as charged."

Her forehead creased. "You're kidding me, right?" She turned the book over and stared at the author's bio on the back. "I always thought you were a woman. Avery is a female name, too."

Avery laughed. "As far as I know, I'm a man."

"There's no author picture on the back. Why not?" Lisa stared up at him expectantly.

"Well, it's probably because I'm not very photogenic," he said. "I'm told I look like a hermit." He winked.

Lisa was horrified. She lifted a hand to cover her face. "I'm so embarrassed. Who told you I call you a hermit?"

Avery laughed. "It doesn't really matter. Besides, I don't blame you. I've acted like a grouchy hermit since I moved in. But I found your description of me rather amusing."

Lisa groaned. "I'm sorry."

"No problem. The truth is my publisher decided not to add a photo on the back. They didn't mean to deceive readers by letting them think I was a woman, but after my first book sold so well, they decided to keep my picture off the covers and let women think I was female. I don't care either way, just as long as I get paid."

Lisa still felt awful about the hermit name. "If it makes you feel any better, I've read several of your books. They're very good." She still couldn't believe this guy she'd always thought was ornery actually wrote tender love stories.

"Thanks." His glance moved to Abby, who'd sat down on the floor and was rubbing her eyes. "It looks like the princess is getting sleepy."

Lisa bent down and lifted her up. "It's time for bed, isn't it, sweetie?"

"No bed," Abby protested, but her heavy lids told a different story.

"Do you mind if I take a look at your backyard while you put her to bed? I mean, if it isn't a problem," he said.

"No. Please go ahead. You can use the door at the end of the hallway. I'll be out in a few minutes."

Lisa watched as Avery made his way down the hall with Bailey following at his heels. This had been a long, extraordinary day. But the biggest surprise had been how quickly she'd softened toward the hermit.

"Ugh!" she said aloud, remembering that Avery now knew what she'd called him.

"Ghug!" Abby said softly, copying her mother.

Lisa laughed. "Come on, little girl. Time for bed."

* * *

Avery walked down the hallway and out the back door with Bailey trotting happily beside him. He noticed that there was a doggie door attached. That explained how he got outside during the day.

Today had been an eye-opener for Avery. He'd had such a bad attitude for so long, he'd forgotten how nice it was to share a meal with a nice woman and enjoy her company. No doubt, Lisa was good-looking. He'd even say beautiful. Her hair had still been up in a messy ponytail and she wore minimal make-up, but she'd looked lovely.

Too bad she thinks I'm a hermit.

He sighed. He couldn't blame her. He'd acted like a crazy hermit these past few months. But he'd had good reason. Being cast aside and taken for a ride by his wife, he found it easy to believe that everyone had an agenda. He'd forgotten what it was like to have friends. Or nice neighbors.

Once he was in Lisa's small backyard, he saw the rocks around the fence. It didn't look bad, but it still hadn't been enough to keep Bailey from digging. He noticed the new hole under the fence. Looking around, he saw a shovel leaning against the back of the house. He grabbed it and began filling in the hole, then pushed a layer of rocks over it.

As he stared at the fence, he had an idea how to stop Bailey from getting out. It might not stop him from digging, but if his plan worked, the dog wouldn't be able to get under the fence.

"It looks like I need to outsmart you, Bailey," he told the dog.

Bailey just wagged his tail and smiled.

Lisa came out wearing a blue sweater over the long-sleeved tee she had on. He noticed how the color of her sweater made her eyes an even deeper blue.

"Did I hear you talking to the dog?" she asked in a teasing tone. "That's the first sign of insanity."

Avery chuckled. "I gave up on being sane years ago. That's why I live in my own head, writing stories."

She laughed. He liked the sound of her laughter. He was pretty sure that Lisa hadn't had much to laugh about over the past few months, other than cute little Abby.

"Any ideas hit you?" she asked.

"Ideas?"

"For the fence," she said.

"Oh, yeah. The fence." Sheesh! He sounded like an idiot. "I do have an idea. I've heard of people burying a strip of chicken wire about two feet below the fence so when the dog digs, he'll be blocked by the wire. Then you can put the rocks over it, too, for added protection."

"That is a good idea." Lisa's face brightened. "And it shouldn't be too costly. It will take some work to dig a trench along the fence line."

"I'd be happy to do it for you, if you'd like," Avery offered. Instantly, he realized what he'd done. He already had a tight deadline for his novel and here he was, offering to spend time digging up her yard and adding wire.

"I couldn't possibly ask you to do that," she said, shaking her head.

Avery wanted to see her smile again. He liked how her face lit up when she smiled. "You didn't ask. I offered."

"Well." She hesitated.

"You won't owe me a thing. I promise. And after the job is done, if you never want to see me around here again, I'll go back to being a hermit."

She bit her lip, obviously still embarrassed. "I'm really sorry for that," she said softly.

He smiled. "Like I said. I don't blame you for thinking of me that way. Maybe we can start over? I promise I'll try to be more congenial than I've been. I'd be happy to fix your fence for you."

"That's very nice of you," she said, her worried expression fading. "And truth be told, I'm relieved that you offered. I'm sure I could do it myself, but it would take weeks. I just don't have the time."

Avery didn't really have the time either, but now that he'd offered so adamantly, he was happy he had. After his terrible behavior toward her, it was the least he could do. "So, is it okay if I come over here tomorrow while you're at work and start on it? I'll pick up the wire in the morning and be here early."

"That'll be fine. I'll give you a key for the lock on the gate. And the money for the wire. Any idea how much it'll cost?" She was already heading back into the house.

"Don't worry about it. You can catch me later on it. But I'll take the key."

She turned, and her eyes looked worried again for a brief moment, but then she nodded and headed into the house to retrieve the key.

Avery glanced down at Bailey, who was sitting beside him on the grass. "Well, bud. It looks like we'll be spending a lot of time together.

Bailey only grinned.

Chapter Six

Avery awoke early the next morning despite having been up late working on his manuscript. His writing was going slowly and felt awkward. He was actually relieved he had a project to do instead. Maybe, as he did the mindless work of digging, he'd be able to work the story out in his head before sitting down to write again.

Maybe.

He dressed in old clothes and headed to a hardware store where he bought a roll of chicken wire and cutters. Then, he was back in his car and arrived at Lisa's house by nine. He knew she'd already left for work, so he helped himself into the backyard. No sooner had he entered the gated area than Bailey was out the doggie door and greeting him.

"Hey there, boy," Avery said, petting his silky coat. The dog bounced around him then ran to fetch a ball so he would play. Avery laughed. He couldn't believe he'd been so mean about Bailey coming over to his house. Well, except for him digging around his bushes. But if Avery had just given the dog a chance, he would have seen he was just a puppy that needed attention.

After throwing the ball for Bailey a few times and trying to teach him how to drop it instead of chasing him for it, Avery got down to work. He used a metal rake to push aside the stones by the fence and began to dig a trench.

The day grew warmer as the sun rose higher in the sky. Avery discarded the flannel shirt he'd been wearing and only wore a white T-shirt underneath. He hadn't worked out in a gym—his gym that he'd given up—in over a year and he felt it in his arms, legs, and back. He was only thirty-six, but after digging for a couple of hours, he felt like he was a hundred.

"Getting thirsty yet?" A female voice interrupted his thoughts. He glanced up and standing on the other side of the fence was the neighbor lady—he assumed this was Kristen—holding out a bottle of water and a small cooler.

"Hi," he said, surprised to see her. "Yeah, I am getting thirsty and I forgot to bring over something to drink."

She handed him the bottle, then lifted the cooler. "I brought you a couple more bottles of water and some lunch. It's only a sandwich, carrots, and chips, but I figured it would fill you up after all the work you've been doing."

He accepted the cooler, stunned that she would take the time to do this for him. "That was very nice of you," he said. "Thank you."

"No problem. I'm Kristen, by the way."

"Avery," he said. "Nice to finally meet you."

"Same here." She smiled.

"Did Lisa tell you I was working on the yard today?" He wondered if Lisa had asked her to bring him lunch.

She shook her head, her thick, auburn hair swaying as she moved. She was a pretty woman and didn't look as ferocious as her husband had made her sound. But then, looks could be deceiving. He'd found that out from his ex-wife.

"I saw you working out here from my kitchen window. It's

nice that you're doing this for Lisa. I figured the least I could do was bring you something for lunch."

Avery had known thoughtful people in his life. Heck, he had even been considered a nice guy once too. But it had been a long time since someone had done something for him without expecting anything in return. "Wow. This is a nice neighborhood," he said without thinking.

Kristen laughed. "It is. If you give it a chance. I'm glad to see that you're trying."

He grinned. "So, does this make us friends? You're not coming to my house to tell me off anytime soon?"

She broke out in laughter. "Is that what Ryan told you? I guess I was a little over-the-top yesterday. But as long as you're nice to Lisa, I'll refrain from yelling at you."

Avery liked Kristen. She was funny and feisty, and just a good person. Both she and Ryan seemed like decent people. He suddenly wished he'd gotten to know them sooner instead of avoiding them.

"That's good to hear," he said. "And thanks for the lunch. I really appreciate it."

"You're welcome. I'd better get back inside. My daughter is napping then we're going for a long walk to the park. I have to get my walks in before winter hits."

He nodded, understanding how their weather could change quickly.

She waved and he did too. Then she disappeared through the hole in the bushes.

Avery decided to take a break. He walked over to the back porch and sat on the top step. Bailey ambled over to him and sat there, watching him.

"I suppose you want me to share," Avery said.

Bailey grinned that goofy dog grin.

Opening the cooler, he pulled out the sandwich, which was wrapped in cellophane. "Looks like ham and swiss on rye," he told Bailey. He unwrapped the sandwich and took a bite. "Perfect."

After sharing a little of the ham with Bailey and eating the rest of his lunch, Avery went back to work. He figured he'd lay down the chicken wire in the trench he'd dug so far then cover it up. Tomorrow he'd dig the second half of the fence line and lay the wire.

Tomorrow. He couldn't remember the last time he'd actually planned something for the next day, other than writing. Since Melissa had left him, he'd basically been floating. His writing had suffered, and he'd had no energy to try anything new. Every day had been the same. Get up, try to write, take a long walk, try to write again, go to bed. But now, he actually felt as if he had something to look forward to.

"Even if it is only digging a hole and laying chicken wire," he said to Bailey. That was when it hit him. If it hadn't been for the rambunctious dog, he wouldn't be here now. He wouldn't have met Lisa properly or even Ryan and Kristen. He cocked his head and stared at Bailey. "Is this what you planned all along?"

Bailey only smiled.

* * *

Lisa walked through her front door, exhausted from her busy day. She set Abby down and the little girl immediately tottered off down the hall calling, "Baywee!"

Lisa sighed, dropped her bags on the floor, and plopped down on the sofa. What a day! Half the children in the school seemed to have come down with a cold at the same time. She'd taken temperatures and called parents all day, praying she wouldn't get whatever the children were passing around. That was the last thing she needed. She didn't want Abby to get sick, either.

Abby. All of a sudden, she sat up, realizing she didn't hear the little girl calling for the dog. And they hadn't come back to the living room as they usually did. She flew off the sofa and hurried down the hall. "Abby!"

Stopping at the back door, she saw Abby on the lawn, trying to throw the ball for Bailey to fetch. *How in the heck did she get outside?* That was when she saw Avery standing over by the fence, watching Abby. She sighed with relief. She'd forgotten he was working on the fence today. She watched as he joined in on the game of fetch. He rolled the ball to Abby, then she rolled it to Bailey. Avery was trying to get Bailey to return the ball so he could roll it to Abby again. Her daughter was laughing and squealing with delight at playing ball with him and Bailey.

The sight of them playing warmed her heart.

Avery looked different today. He was wearing dirty jeans and a white T-shirt that clung to his chest, probably from sweat. Until this moment, she hadn't realized how muscular he was. He'd always hid it under a loose shirt when he'd come over to complain. Now, he looked absolutely hunky.

Sheesh. Get a grip on yourself.

At that exact moment, he glanced up and spied her standing in the doorway. He smiled and waved, and she felt guilty for having been standing there, ogling him. She walked outside to join them.

"Hi. It looks like you've accomplished a lot today," she said, trying hard not to stare at his arms and chest. Up close, she could see the outline of his muscles.

"Yeah. I was just filling in the dirt on this half that I finished. I'll rake the rocks back over it, too. I figured tomorrow I'd finish the other half."

"That sounds good," she said. When he smiled at her, she was suddenly self-conscious that she must look a wreck. Her ponytail had loosened throughout the day and she'd never had a chance to fix it. Strands of hair fell in her face. And make-up? She doubted the little she wore was still on her face after nine hours of rushing around.

Why do I care what he thinks? She smoothed the hair back from her face, but to no avail. It fell down again anyway.

"I hope you don't mind my letting Abby out here to play with Bailey. She was at the door, calling him. He's been by my side all day," Avery said.

"No, I don't mind. She loves playing outside with Bailey. And we might as well enjoy the nice weather while we still have it, right?"

He nodded. "Well, I'll just finish raking the rocks here then be out of your way." He turned back to his work by the fence.

As Lisa watched him move the rocks with the rake, she considered inviting him to stay for dinner. But she wasn't sure what she'd serve. She still had the jar of soup that Kristen had given her, but would that be enough for the three of them? She could order something to be delivered, but that was costly, and she was watching her pennies.

Maybe I should just forget it and let him go home.

The more she thought of it, though, the more she wanted his company for dinner. It had been fun having an adult to eat with last night. Someone other than Abby to actually have a conversation with. And besides, he was fixing her fence. Shouldn't she pay back the favor?

"Well, maybe I'll see you tomorrow," he said, leaning the rake against the fence and grabbing his flannel shirt.

Without giving it another thought, she blurted out, "Would you like to have dinner with us tonight? I mean, it's the least I can do after all the work you're doing for me."

Avery studied her a moment. "You don't have to feel obligated to feed me. I don't mind fixing the fence for you."

She cringed, realizing that her offer had sounded more like an obligation than an invitation. "I didn't mean it to sound that way. I'd be happy to have you over for dinner, if you'd like to come. It won't be anything fancy, just homemade soup and grilled cheese sandwiches."

He smiled. "I like grilled cheese sandwiches. Thanks. I'd like to eat with you and Abby again." He looked down at his dirty clothes. "But I think I'd better go change first. I'll be back soon, okay?"

She nodded. "That's fine. See you in a bit."

As soon as Avery left, Lisa scooped up Abby and called Bailey inside. "We have to clean up a little," she told Abby. "We have company for dinner tonight." The thought of Avery joining them made Lisa smile.

An hour later they were all sitting around the dining room table eating chicken noodle soup and grilled cheese sandwiches along with a few cut-up veggies and dip. Lisa had hastily changed into jeans and a T-shirt and combed her hair, leaving it down. She'd also added a little concealer to cover up the dark circles under her eyes and a swipe of mascara. It was the best she could do in the little time she'd had. She knew she shouldn't care how she looked around Avery, but despite that, she did care.

She was surprised when he'd arrived freshly showered and smelling delicious from a spicy aftershave. She wasn't sure if she should be flattered he'd gone to the trouble to look nice or if she should be wary that he thought this was more than just an offer of dinner.

Oh, heck. Get over yourself.

"This soup is good," Avery said. "You said it was homemade?"

"Yes, but I didn't make it. I'd never have the time to do that. Kristen did. She makes a different soup almost every week and always gives me a jar. Everything she makes is good."

"I believe that," he said. "She was kind enough to bring me a couple of water bottles and make me lunch. I was stunned at her thoughtfulness. She's pretty amazing."

"Wow. She brought you lunch? That's great. It just shows you why I love this neighborhood so much. Everyone helps each other."

They ate their simple meal and talked about easy things like her day at work and how he was trying to teach Bailey to fetch and drop a ball. Avery asked Abby what she'd done that day and although Lisa doubted he understood half of what the toddler said, he was attentive and nodded like he did. She thought that was sweet. He seemed comfortable with children and definitely with dogs. She liked that.

After they'd eaten, Lisa was surprised that she didn't want him to leave. But Abby needed a bath that night and she'd taken up enough of his writing time. She walked him to the door as Abby played with toys on the living room floor and Bailey watched.

"I'm glad you stayed for dinner. It's nice having another adult to talk to for a change," she said.

"Ah, so that was why you invited me. You used me for my ability to string words together." He grinned, then said more seriously, "Thank you for inviting me. I've been eating too many meals alone. And too much junk food. I also enjoyed having someone to talk to."

She smiled. It was hard to believe that just yesterday she couldn't stand him. Now, it was like they were old friends. "Well, then. I'll see you tomorrow after work."

He nodded, waved, and headed down the sidewalk and across the street. She watched him go, a little longer than she'd meant to. Before he went inside his house, he turned and saw her watching him, waved again, and went inside.

Lisa quickly shut the door. "Crap!" He'd seen her watching him. What must he be thinking?

"Cap!" Abby said behind her.

Lisa laughed. "Come on, you little monkey. Let's go play in the bath."

Chapter Seven

Avery sat in front of his laptop trying to concentrate on his writing. After coming home from Lisa's, he'd changed into sweats before heading to his office. His muscles ached from working all day, but it actually felt good. It was nice being outside in the sunshine, doing physical labor. He'd been sitting in front of a computer for too long, not getting the exercise he needed. But now, he had to get to work at his own job. Unfortunately, he couldn't keep his mind on his fictional characters. Instead, he kept thinking about Lisa.

He looked across the street and saw her light was still on in the living room. Avery smiled. He'd had such a good time eating with her and Abby again. Abby was adorable and he'd enjoyed watching her try to manipulate her fork and spoon so she could be like a "big girl," as she put it. But more than that, he was warmed by the look of pure love on Lisa's face every time she looked at her daughter. She practically glowed with love and pride.

Had he ever loved anyone as much as Lisa loved Abby? Had anyone loved him that way?

"Well, maybe my mother," he mumbled to himself. "But definitely not Melissa." She'd never looked at him with that kind of adoration in her eyes. Maddie had looked at him that way, though. But then, she was a dog.

He truly missed his Maddie.

He'd found it cute how Lisa was still watching him as he crossed the street and turned at his door. Even at that distance, he could see her startled expression because she'd been caught. He didn't mind that Lisa had been watching him. In fact, it had boosted his ego a notch—something he desperately needed.

Refocusing on his computer screen, Avery began to type. Then he hit delete. Then he typed again. Delete. *Cripes! What is wrong with me?* Writing love stories was his thing. Why was this one so difficult?

He looked over his notes, read the character descriptions, and tried to get a feel for the story again. It was about a successful woman whose husband had died ten years before. Then she meets a guy she feels she could fall in love with. He's rich and charming, but the more she gets to know him, the more she realizes that she will never find another man she adores as much as her husband. Is she destined to be alone forever, never to have children of her own? What she doesn't realize is her good friend at her office is really the man of her dreams. But she doesn't see it. Because sometimes the thing you want most isn't out in the distance; it's right in front of you.

Solid story. So why can't I just write it?

Glancing at the clock, he saw it was ten. He looked out the window again. Lisa's lights were out. "I am stalking her," he said aloud, disgusted with himself. He pulled the shade so he wouldn't be distracted anymore and forced himself to type.

He gazed into her ~~bright blue eyes~~ warm brown eyes and watched as she pushed back her silky ~~golden~~ black hair from her face. Her full, pink lips were inviting as she raised her face to his.

"I've never met anyone like you," he said huskily, drawing close enough to smell her sweet scent of lilacs ~~and baby lotion~~. He gently touched the side of her face as he lowered his lips to hers. A delicious kiss. A satisfying kiss that he felt deep down into his soul and never wanted to end.

Avery stopped writing. He wasn't thinking about the characters as he wrote, he was thinking of Lisa.

Frustrated, he closed his computer, turned out the light, and headed to bed.

* * *

Friday morning Avery once again went to Lisa's yard to finish working. This time, he brought a cooler with water and lunch. When Kristen came outside with her little girl to get into her car, he waved and pointed at his cooler.

"Glad you remembered today," she called. "I have a few appointments to run to. Have a good day."

"You, too," he called back.

He moved the rocks and dug a new trench along the other half of the fence. Then he cut the chicken wire and began laying it, making sure it overlapped with the chain link fencing. As he worked, he thought about his novel and tried to work out the details in his head. He knew exactly what he wanted to write, but it just wouldn't come out that way.

"Maybe I should come up with a different storyline," he told Bailey, who'd lain down in the shade near him. "This one might be too overdone, and that's why I can't get excited about it."

The dog cocked his head but didn't share any words of wisdom.

By noon, Avery was hot, and his muscles ached. He sat down

on the steps to eat his lunch as he'd done yesterday. There was a big oak tree overhead and it shaded the area. Halfway through eating, he heard his phone buzz. He winced when he saw it was his agent.

"Hey, Jackson. How are you?" Avery said, sounding more chipper than he felt. He knew exactly why Jackson was calling and didn't have a good answer for him.

"I'm just fine," Jackson McAfee said. "What about you?"

"Can't complain," Avery said.

"Well, that would be a first," Jackson said, then laughed. "You've done nothing but complain over the past year."

Avery sobered. He knew it was the truth but didn't like being reminded of it. "What's up, Jackson?"

"I'm just checking on you. How is that new novel coming along? It feels like you're pushing it close to the wire with this one. Usually, I'd have several chapters on my desk by now."

Avery sighed. He wished he had several chapters completed. "I know. This one is giving me trouble. Quite frankly, this past year has been nothing but a pain."

"I get it. It's been tough for you. But you managed to finish your last novel and edit it on time during your breakup and divorce. What's holding you back now?"

A crease formed between Avery's brows. "Yeah, I did. But it was tough then, and it still is. I'm working as hard as I can."

"I believe you," Jackson said, his tone kinder. "I'm just a little worried about you and your new manuscript. You have less than a month to turn it in and I haven't seen any of it."

"I know." Avery paused. He'd been thinking about this for a while but had really believed he could make the deadline. Now, he wasn't sure. "Listen, Jackson. I was wondering if we could extend the due date by a few weeks. I know that's not always easy, but I need more time."

There was silence on the other end of the line. Avery knew that Jackson didn't like the idea of an extension. But in the six years he'd been writing for this particular publisher, he'd never been late. Surely they could give him a break just once.

"I hate breaking a contract," Jackson finally said. "Especially since your last book didn't sell as well as expected."

Avery stiffened. He hated when sales were thrown in his face as a way to control him. "Sales would have been fine if they'd advertised my book more. And even so, the sales weren't as bad as all that. I'd think that after all the money I've made for them, and you, over the years, I should be allowed to have one extension."

"I see," Jackson said tightly. "You don't have to get nasty about it. I'll contact them and see what they feel will be appropriate. How much time do you think you'll need?"

A year or two, Avery thought. But he knew he couldn't say that. "Two months."

Jackson let out a long breath. "Okay. I can always ask, but I can't promise they'll agree. If I were you, I'd work night and day to finish it as soon as possible."

Avery gave a short laugh. "Yeah. As if it's that easy. If the story was going that well, I'd be done with it already."

They talked for another couple of minutes then Avery hung up. Agents! They just didn't get it. Publishers didn't get it either. Sometimes you couldn't just push out a story on demand. If he could, he'd be a lot richer than he was.

He turned to the dog. "Okay, Bailey. Break's over. At least I know I can finish this project today." Avery stood and stretched his back. He suddenly realized that once he was finished, he wouldn't have a good reason to come over here anymore. That thought bothered him.

He rubbed Bailey behind the ears, getting a smile in return, then went back to the fence to work.

* * *

Halfway through her day, Lisa realized it was Friday. And not just any Friday, it was one of the two weekends a month that Andrew was allowed to take Abby for the weekend.

She hated the weekends he took her. She knew divorced parents who enjoyed the time away from their children, but she didn't. Lisa felt Abby was too young to be shuffled around. True, Andrew was good with her and truly loved his daughter, but he didn't spend enough time with her to know her well. And it didn't help that Andrew's live-in girlfriend, Katrina Meyers, wasn't exactly a kid person. Lisa wrinkled her nose at the thought of Katrina with her stiff, bleached-blond hair, thick coat of make-up, and too-tight clothes. It seemed she had no interest in a busy little girl like Abby. She wouldn't even hold her because she didn't want to get her clothes dirty.

Lisa looked down at her stained top with Disney characters printed on it and laughed. Getting dirty around kids all day just happened. She certainly didn't have a problem with it.

After school let out, Lisa rushed to get Abby from the day care next door and hurried home. She had to make sure Abby had a snack—because God only knew what Andrew would feed her for dinner—and was in a clean outfit, packed, and ready to go by five-thirty. Andrew was always promptly on time. If he had to wait even a minute, he'd comment again on it being yet another reason he wanted joint custody, and Lisa didn't want to argue about that. They had a court date set for next month where the judge would decide, and she didn't want to give Andrew any new ammunition to bolster his case. Her lawyer from legal aid had said she shouldn't worry—judges still tended to side with the mother—but that didn't make her feel any more secure. She knew the only reason Andrew wanted full joint custody was because he wanted to lower the amount of child support he paid her. She also knew for certain that he wouldn't take Abby for more than a weekend here or there despite joint custody, but he'd be paying her less. She needed that money to keep afloat and any reduction would make life even more difficult.

It truly upset her that children were used as bargaining chips in a divorce.

When they'd first separated, he'd agreed she should have full custody of Abby and they'd set the terms for his visits. With a new girlfriend in his life, he hadn't wanted the burden of caring for Abby half the time. Lisa had been relieved, because she hadn't wanted Abby tossed weekly between two households. Once he'd learned what his child support payments would be, his tune had changed. Every time she thought of it, she grew angry.

Lisa arrived at the house and let Abby run down the hall to call for Bailey. Hurriedly, she packed a bag for her daughter with all her necessities and favorite toys. She was almost finished when she heard footsteps in the hallway. Heavy footsteps. A shadow fell over her from the doorway. Startled, she turned quickly and nearly fell back on the toddler's bed.

"You scared me to death!" she said, placing her hand over her heart.

Avery looked worried. "I'm sorry. I didn't mean to scare you. I just wanted to ask if it was okay for Abby to come outside with me again."

Lisa sighed. Thinking how ridiculous she must have looked to him, she began laughing. It released the tension she'd been feeling all afternoon.

"Uh, are you okay?" Avery asked, taking another step inside the room. From behind him, Abby peeked around his legs.

That only made Lisa laugh harder. "I'm fine. I was so intent on what I was doing, I'd forgotten you might be in the backyard."

Avery smiled. "Sorry."

"No problem. And yes, she can go out for a little while, but then I need to give her a snack before she leaves."

His brows rose. "Leaves? Is she running away from home or something?"

She grinned. "No. Her father is picking her up for the weekend. He takes her every other weekend."

"Daddy," Abby said softly.

"Yes, sweetie," Lisa said, turning to Abby. "Daddy will be here soon." Lisa noticed the smile on Avery's face had faded.

"Okay then." He offered Abby his hand. "Let's go see what Bailey's up to."

The little girl smiled brightly up at him and happily took his hand. Lisa watched as they walked down the hall to go outside.

Something tugged at her heart. Something about Avery and Abby, holding hands.

"It's sweet," she said quietly. She hadn't expected sweet from a hermit.

Promptly at five-thirty, the doorbell rang. Bailey barked and danced around, causing Lisa to have to pull him away from the door. She opened it, and there stood Andrew in his three-piece suit and polished shoes, clean shaven, and not one brown hair out of place. In the car was Katrina, carefully applying lipstick.

Lisa cringed. She hadn't so much as looked in the mirror when she came home. She must have looked a fright.

"Hi, Lisa. Is Abby ready?" He peered around her to where

Abby was sitting with her toys on the living room floor with Bailey circling her.

"Yeah. Come on in. I'll get her bag." Lisa moved aside so he could step in. Instantly, Bailey ran over and jumped on him.

Andrew angrily pushed the dog away. "Get back! Get down, you stupid dog."

Lisa tried not to smile. *Jump some more,* she secretly thought. *Ruin that fancy suit of his.*

"Baywee!" Abby called excitedly. By the time Lisa came back from the bedroom with the bag, Bailey was once again near his favorite little person and Andrew was brushing off invisible dirt from his suit.

"You should train that dog," he grumbled.

"He's just a puppy," Lisa said, handing him Abby's bag. "And remember, you're the one who brought him here."

Andrew studied her a moment, seemingly ready with a mean retort when a voice came from the hallway.

"He's a smart dog. He'll learn as soon as he can retain it. Most obedience schools won't even train a dog until it's over six months old."

Lisa saw Avery standing at the end of the hallway and smiled. His T-shirt and jeans were stained with dirt and his hair was mussed. But at this very moment, she thought he was a hero for talking back to Andrew.

"And who are you?" Andrew asked, sneering at Avery.

Avery ignored him and looked at Lisa. "Sorry to interrupt. I just came in to tell you I'm finished out back. I'll put the leftover wire and the shovel in the garage."

"Thanks, Avery," she said.

Andrew frowned. "Who's he? The gardener? I guess you're living pretty well if you can afford to pay a gardener."

Anger rushed through Lisa's veins. "No. He's not a gardener. He was helping secure the fence so Bailey wouldn't dig another hole and crawl under it. Believe me, I don't have an extra dime, let alone money to pay a gardener."

Andrew regarded her for a moment, then decided to stay silent. He walked over to Abby. "Come on, Abbs. It's time to go." He bent down and picked up his daughter.

"Mommy?" she asked, her bottom lip starting to quiver.

Lisa's heart twisted. This happened every time. Abby was at an age when it scared her to be away from her mom, and she really didn't spend enough time with her dad to know him well. Lisa stepped over beside Andrew and gently ran her hand up and down Abby's back. "It's okay, sweetie. You're going to Daddy's for the weekend. You'll have a lot of fun." She kissed her on the cheek, but a tear was already falling.

"Baywee!" Abby called, more tears coming.

"Maybe she'd feel better if Bailey came along, too," Lisa said.

"Are you crazy? Katrina would have a fit. Abby will be fine. She always cries for the first few minutes then she has a good time."

Lisa hated this every time it happened. She knew Andrew was a good parent, when he was around, but hearing Abby cry as he took her away was always gut-wrenching. She watched as Andrew took her out to the car and buckled her into her car seat. She could hear her daughter wailing. Tears filled Lisa's eyes as she listened. Finally, Andrew shut the door and drove off. But she stood, rooted to the spot, long after they'd driven away.

Chapter Eight

Avery was walking down Lisa's driveway to the front yard when he saw Andrew slam his car door and drive away.

Gardener! Right! Stupid guy in his fancy three-piece suit. Probably hasn't ever gotten his hands dirty a day in his life. I could afford to buy a fancy suit too, if I wanted to look like a jerk.

He didn't know why he disliked the guy so much, but he did. Of course, over the past year, Avery hadn't liked practically everyone.

As he came to the front yard, he noticed Lisa standing on the front porch, her head in her hands. On impulse, he sprinted up the steps. "Are you okay?"

Lisa raised her head, blue eyes full of tears as droplets streamed down her face. The pained look she gave him made him instantly want to comfort her. He moved closer, hesitating for only a moment. Then he wrapped his arms around her and pulled her into his chest. She didn't resist. Her tears came faster as her shoulders shook. The harder she cried, the tighter he hugged her.

They stood together for a long while, neither of them aware of anything else around them but each other. They were so close, her hair tickled his face. She smelled like lilacs and baby lotion.

He would have found that humorous if she hadn't been so upset. He knew he must smell terrible after working in the sun all day, and his clothes were filthy. But she didn't seem to mind. She curled into him and held on as if she were drowning.

After a time, Lisa's tears slowed, and she pulled back a little. As he gazed into her eyes, he had a deep desire to kiss her. He wanted to kiss her in a way that made her forget whatever it was that had caused her to cry. But, with difficulty, he refrained. This definitely wasn't the right time.

"I'm sorry," she said, pulling away. "I never fall apart like that." She dropped her eyes and then said, "At least not in public."

"You don't have to be sorry," he told her. "We all have our moments."

She nodded. When she raised her eyes again, she managed to give him a small smile. "Thank you. You're not too bad for a hermit."

He laughed a warm, deep chuckle, and she joined in.

"Why don't I buy you dinner?" he asked, hoping he wasn't treading on shaky ground. "Something casual. There's a pub not far from here that's good." He watched as she took a breath and hesitated. *She's going to say no,* he thought, regretfully.

"Shouldn't I be the one to take you out for dinner?" she asked. "After all, you just spent two days fixing my fence, and the last few minutes trying to fix me."

A strand of hair fell down the side of her face, and Avery had the urge to slip it behind her ear with his finger. A character in his books would do that. It was an intimate, romantic gesture. But it was too personal for their relationship at this moment. He shoved his hands in his pockets. "It's my night to buy," he said. "You made dinner last night."

Again, she hesitated, then gave him a smile. "Sure. It might be nice to get out of the house for a change." She looked down at her clothes. "I'll need to clean up a bit, though."

"Me, too," he said. "Meet you at seven? I'll drive my car over."

She nodded. With a wave, she went inside and closed the door.

Avery couldn't help but smile the entire way home.

* * *

"What have I done? Is this a date?" Lisa stared at herself in the bathroom mirror. "Have I agreed to a date with Avery?" Suddenly, panic set in. She couldn't believe she'd just stood there on the porch, crying in Avery's arms. Hearing Abby sobbing had torn her apart. It had happened before, but Lisa had been able to soldier through it. She didn't have much choice. Andrew was allowed the two weekends a month. But this time, it had just been too much.

And then Avery had held her, and slowly, she'd felt better.

"I look like a crazy person." Something cold and wet touched her hand, startling her. She looked down and there sat Bailey, looking sad.

Kneeling, Lisa petted the dog's head. "Sorry, boy. I know you miss Abby when she's gone. It's only for a couple of days." She stood again and took another look at herself. "Well, Bailey. I have a lot of work to do in the next hour."

Bailey lay down next to her and, luckily, didn't agree.

Right at seven, the doorbell rang. Lisa slipped on a pair of flats and headed for the door, a sweater hanging over the crook of her arm. It had taken her fifteen minutes to decide what to wear, and in the end, she'd stuck with jeans, a white shirt, black flats, and a red sweater for later when the night air cooled. She hoped she wouldn't look too casual, like she didn't care. Did she care? She didn't know.

Opening the door, she almost sighed with relief. Avery was wearing jeans too, a loose shirt, and cowboy boots. "Hi," she said, suddenly feeling shy.

"Hi." He smiled. "You ready?"

"Yep. I'll grab my purse."

Bailey had come over to inspect Avery too. The dog grew excited and started bouncing around, but when Avery put his hand down, palm flat, Bailey stopped and sat.

Lisa watched in amazement. "How did you do that?"

"I taught him the command while I was working on the fence. He's a smart dog, like I told your ex. You just have to know how to handle him."

Lisa grinned. "So, you could have stopped Bailey from jumping on Andrew's suit?"

He grinned back. "Probably."

They both laughed, said goodbye to Bailey, and headed out the door to Avery's SUV. The pub was only three blocks away and Avery parked close by.

"I've seen this place, but I've never eaten here," Lisa said as they stepped out of the car. "It's so close, we could have walked."

"We could have, but it'll be dark by the time we leave. I didn't think we should walk in the dark," Avery said.

"Are you afraid of the dark?" she teased.

"No. Hermits aren't afraid of the dark." He winked.

"I'll never live that one down, will I?"

"Not if I can help it." He grinned and opened the door to the pub, letting her enter ahead of him.

Since it was a Friday night, the place was crowded, but they managed to find a table in the back where it wasn't as noisy.

The pub was small, with dark wood floors, tables, and wainscoting, and hunter-green wallpaper on the upper part of the walls. Antique advertising signs decorated the cozy space.

"This reminds me of Gallagher's," Lisa said. "Only smaller."

Avery nodded. "I suppose all Irish pubs sort of look alike. Except they don't all have Gallagher's great hamburgers."

The waitress came over and took their drink order, leaving menus. Lisa opened her menu but noticed Avery didn't. "Do you eat here so often you don't even have to look at the menu?"

"Yes and no. I guess I come here once a week. Mostly, I order pizza delivered to the house. Like, almost every night." He grimaced.

"How do you stay in shape eating all that pizza?"

One eyebrow rose. "You think I'm in shape?"

Lisa felt her face heat up. "I mean, well, you don't look overweight or anything." *Great. Now he thinks I was checking him out.*

Avery laughed. "I was just teasing you. I take long walks almost every day, but I wish I still had my home gym. I miss working out."

She was just about to ask him about his home gym when the waitress came back. She set down Lisa's red wine and Avery's beer. Lisa ordered the grilled chicken salad and Avery said he'd have a cheeseburger.

The waitress winked at him. "The usual, right?"

"Yeah. I suppose. Creature of habit."

Lisa watched as the waitress headed toward the bar. The woman was at least ten years younger than Avery, but it looked like she'd been flirting with him. "She seems to know you well."

Avery looked confused. "The waitress? Not really. Like I said, I come here once a week. She just knows what I order." He cocked his head. "Why? Are you jealous?"

"No. Why would I be jealous? I don't care who you date. Even if she is way too young for you." Lisa stopped, realizing how snitty that sounded. But Avery was grinning at her.

"Too young, huh? Well, I have to agree with you. My wife was younger than me, and I paid dearly for that. No more younger women for me. Besides, I can't keep up with them. I'm too old."

"I didn't mean it that way," she said, feeling contrite.

"I know," he said. "Is that what happened between you and your husband? He found someone younger? I mean, you don't look a day over twenty-five, so I'm not sure how he found someone else younger and still of legal age."

She chuckled. "I'm thirty-two. And no. She wasn't younger, just easier."

"Easier?"

"Oops. I didn't mean that kind of easier, although, if the shoe fits. No, she was single and free to go running around to bars and didn't have a baby to contend with. I think Andrew started feeling too tied down with the house and Abby, and, well, was looking for fun again." She shrugged. "I don't really understand it. He wanted to buy the house and he wanted me to stay home with Abby after she was born. But then he resented it after a while. I thought we were both on the same page, but I guess we weren't."

"I'm sorry. Relationships are hard and they never make sense. I know how that is."

"Do you want to share what happened to your marriage?" she asked.

"I don't mind. Like you, I'm not sure what happened. I thought we had a great marriage. We traveled a lot, had a beautiful home, and we had the freedom to come and go as we pleased.

I thought we were happy. Melissa, my ex, always complained when I'd have to work, but someone had to earn the money. And she said I could be too serious and boring sometimes. Can you imagine that? Me? Boring?" He laughed, and so did Lisa. "So sometimes when I'd work late writing, she'd go out with girlfriends. I never thought anything of it, until she slapped me with divorce papers and said she'd found someone else."

"Wow. That must have been a shock. At least with Andrew, I sort of saw it coming. We were arguing a lot and he was pulling away. By the time we separated, I wasn't too surprised. But I was surprised that he already had a girlfriend and was moving in with her."

"Yeah. Melissa did the same. She found a guy who makes triple what I do, and my income wasn't that shabby. I began to think that she'd always been in it for the money. That can sour a guy on relationships pretty quickly."

The waitress brought their food then left again. They both began to eat. Someone started the jukebox and a country song filled the room.

"How's your salad?" Avery asked.

"It's good." She listened to the song a moment. "So, is this your kind of music? Country?"

Avery looked confused. "Why do you ask that?"

"The boots. You're wearing cowboy boots."

He smiled. "Oh, those. Yeah, I do like country music. But I like older rock, too. What about you?"

"I'm more of a pop music gal. Older rock is good, too. Country, though, is depressing."

Avery shook his head. "That's a shame. I guess that means we can't hang out together anymore."

"Is not liking country music a deal breaker?" she teased.

"Could be."

They ate in silence a moment. Comfortable silence. Lisa liked that. Avery surprised her. Three days ago, she'd thought he was a grouchy, mean, old man. Old! He wasn't any of those things. He was a good-looking guy with a great sense of humor. And he seemed decent. After all, not many men would let a woman they hardly knew cry on their chest like she had today. Nor would just any guy fix her fence. He kept surprising her.

They talked a little more about different subjects. He asked about her job, and she told him funny stories about the things the kids did. When she asked how his writing was going, he brushed the subject aside. "It's all really boring," he told her. He didn't order another beer but drank water the rest of the night and she was glad. It showed he was a careful drinker.

After their plates were cleared away and Lisa thought they'd talked themselves out, Avery spoke up.

"Ryan gave me a good idea that I'd like to run by you. Would you mind if I took Bailey out with me when I walked? I could teach him how to heel and he could get some exercise. He really needs that at his young age."

"You wouldn't mind?" Once again, he'd surprised her with this thoughtful gesture.

"No, not at all. And it might tire him out enough, so he won't try to come up with another way to escape. Especially since I didn't put wire on the opposite side of the yard."

"I figured with all the trees and bushes there, he wouldn't dig," Lisa said. "At least, that's what I'm hoping." She hated the thought of digging up around that fence and adding chicken wire. It might kill the plants and trees.

"Hopefully he won't. So, it's okay if I walk Bailey?"

"Sure. That would be great."

Avery paid the bill and drove her home. He walked her up to the porch, even after she'd said he didn't have to. "This was fun. Thanks for going out with me tonight."

"Thanks for inviting me," she said. "And for dinner. It was great." Lisa unlocked her door and stood there. She wasn't sure what else to say. It had been a wonderful evening and she hated for it to end, which again, surprised her.

"Well," he said, looking unsure of himself too.

"Thanks for letting me cry on you today. I'm sorry you got pulled into all of that."

He moved closer, gazing down into her eyes. "I'm glad I was here. No one should ever cry alone."

His nearness made her nervous. Would he kiss her? Did she want him to? "I can see now why you write romance novels," she teased. "You know how to say the right thing."

This brought a grin on his face. She liked when he smiled. His face was much more handsome with a smile on it.

"Say?" he asked huskily.

"Yes?"

"If you're not doing anything tomorrow, would you like to go walking?"

This completely threw Lisa. She'd thought he was going to ask if he could kiss her. "Um. Well, other than laundry, I guess I'm not doing anything. Yeah. I'd like to go walking."

"Good. Maybe around one? We could go to Lake Harriet and walk the trail. Maybe bring Bailey, too."

"Sure. That would be fun," Lisa said.

"Great. See you tomorrow." Avery gave a little wave and walked back to his car.

"Goodnight," she called after him, still a bit stunned. She went inside and closed the door behind her. Bailey came barreling toward her, ready to jump. Lisa put out her hand the way Avery had done, and the dog stopped in his tracks and sat down.

"It works," she said. Yes indeed. Avery was full of surprises.

Chapter Nine

For the first time in months, Avery felt happy. Not just a little happy but floating-on-air kind of happy. He'd enjoyed spending time with Lisa and felt comfortable with her. Comfortable enough to share about his marriage and divorce, which he hadn't spoken about to anyone over the past year. She understood him. She was going through the same thing. It was nice to finally have someone he could talk to.

He slipped into comfortable clothes and headed to his office. His great night made him excited about working on his novel again. But as he reread some of what he'd last written, he frowned. The writing was stilted. The story was boring. It was a terrible book.

What was he going to do?

He needed a new story. A better story. A story about loss and anger and redemption. A story in which love came slowly, and the woman wasn't the one being saved by the man. Instead, the man would be saved by the woman.

A story like the one beginning between him and Lisa.

He closed the current file and opened a new document, then fervently began writing notes, creating new characters, and even adding a dog. The story forming underneath his fingertips was fleshing out. It was strong. It was real. It was so much better than the one he'd been writing.

Avery smiled. He couldn't wait for tomorrow so he could spend the day with Lisa. But tonight, he wrote.

* * *

Saturday morning Avery was up and showered early, then headed to his keyboard again. He wrote all morning, not wanting to break the flow of words. The characters were fun and witty and real. He liked how they teased each other, and he felt what they felt when they hurt. It was the most honest thing he'd ever written. He knew it as the words filled the pages. And it felt amazing.

A few minutes before one, he slipped on his sneakers and a sweatshirt and filled a small backpack with water bottles and protein bars. As an afterthought, he grabbed Maddie's old leash in case Lisa didn't have one for Bailey. Then he headed across the street to her house.

Lisa opened the front door just as he stepped on the porch. "Hey, there. We're ready to go."

"Great. I wasn't sure if you had a leash, so I brought one," he told her, dropping his backpack and pulling it out.

"Wow. You're a serious walker. A backpack and everything." She looked impressed.

"I wasn't sure how long we'd walk. It doesn't hurt to be prepared."

"No. I think it's great. And your leash looks sturdier than the small one I have, so let's use it. Thanks for thinking of that," Lisa said.

He smiled, pleased with himself for bringing it. As he snapped the leash on Bailey, he thought: *This is going to be a great day.*

They strolled to the end of the block, turned left, then turned right at the next block. Their homes were only eight blocks away from Lake Harriet and they passed through neighborhoods similar to their own with older homes built between 1920 and 1950. Charming streets with old trees that shaded the sidewalks and an array of house styles from Craftsman, bungalow, and Tudor to Victorian and farmhouse. It wasn't until they were across the street from the lake that the houses became larger and more refined, mansions built by the rich from the early 1900s who wanted a view of the lake and to impress their peers.

"I love these old mansions on this street," Lisa said as they moved along the sidewalk, sidestepping Bailey who was darting between them. "They're so beautiful."

Avery grinned as he attempted maneuvering Bailey to stay on his left side and walk in a straight line. "And expensive," he said.

"I'm sure they are. More than I could ever afford."

They continued down the block and Avery suddenly stopped. Bailey and Lisa stopped short too. Avery had been staring at one of the big houses and he couldn't believe what he was seeing.

"What's the matter?" Lisa asked. She glanced around, confused.

Avery felt his blood boil as he stared at a For Sale sign in front of the house. "I can't believe it! How dare she?"

"How dare who?" Lisa asked, still looking around.

Avery pointed. "That 'For Sale' sign. That conniving little witch took my house and now she's selling it. Can she get any lower?"

Lisa's gaze followed to where he was pointing. She turned to Avery and suddenly her face showed comprehension. "Was that your house?"

"Yes. It was. Until she took it from me in the divorce settlement even though I was the one who earned the money to buy it. She swore she had to have it. And now, she's selling it." He mumbled some four-letter words, then remembered who he was with. "Sorry. Let's keep walking."

Avery took off at a fast clip, turned toward the walking path along the lake, then continued his angry stride.

"Avery. Wait up. This was supposed to be a fun walk, not a sprint," Lisa called, running to catch up with him.

He stopped walking, trying hard to push down his anger. He couldn't believe it. He'd loved that house. He'd worked hard to have a home that nice. And now some stranger was going to get it.

When he saw the exasperation on Lisa's face as she caught up, his anger abated. Instead, he felt remorseful. "I'm sorry, Lisa. I shouldn't have acted like that. I'm just so shocked at seeing my old house for sale. I know it's just a house, but it was *my* house. And she's tossing it away like old garbage."

Lisa moved closer to him and placed a hand on his arm. "I get it. And it's not just a house. It was your home. You have a right to be angry." She turned and looked at the house again. "It's beautiful. I'd be angry if someone took it away from me."

He softened as he stared at Lisa. She looked so cute, with her hair up in its usual ponytail, her skin soft and pink from rushing after him. She was beautiful. He wondered if she knew just how beautiful she was. "Thanks for understanding." He glanced down at Bailey, who was sitting next to him, watching other walkers pass them. "Come on. Let's keep walking. I'll burn off my aggravation."

"Are you sure? We can go back if you'd rather," Lisa said.

"I'm absolutely sure. I'd rather be out here with you and Bailey than sitting in my house, stewing." He wrapped an arm around her waist as if it were the most natural thing for him to do.

Lisa smiled widely. "Sounds good."

The day was beautiful. The sun was shining, and the temperature was cool enough that they didn't get overheated. The leaves on the trees were just beginning to turn color, but it would be a few more weeks before they peaked. Avery put his energy into teaching Bailey how to heel as they strode along the path. He shortened the leash at first so Bailey would stay close to him, then said, "Heel," as they walked. Bailey, however, was too intrigued by the other walkers, runners, and bikers, and didn't listen very well.

"It'll take a while before he gets the idea," he told Lisa. "But it's a good start."

The trail was nearly three miles long, so they strolled at a leisurely pace so as not to tire out. Halfway along the trail, they sat on a bench to drink water. Avery offered Lisa a protein bar.

"Wow. You do think of everything," she said, accepting it.

He pulled a small bowl out of the pack and filled it with water for Bailey. The dog happily lapped it up.

"I used to run with my dog on this trail," he told Lisa. "So I was always prepared with water for her."

"You had a dog? What happened to her?" Lisa asked.

Avery sighed. "My ex happened. She got the house, the dog, and pretty much everything else. She didn't even like the dog. She took Maddie to hurt me."

"That's terrible! She does sound like a witch," Lisa said, her face growing red with anger.

Avery chuckled. "Yep. I'm not just making it up. So, you can see why I was so unsociable this past year. After what she did to me, I didn't trust anyone. I wanted to wallow in my misery."

"I guess we all have our issues. Andrew changed his mind after we'd settled on custody for Abby when he found out how much he had to pay for child support. Now, he's taking me back to court to get joint legal and physical custody so he can pay less. I'm hoping that he doesn't really want to take Abby more than every other weekend, but I also can't live on less money. It's scary."

Avery frowned. "That's awful. Does your lawyer think Andrew will win?"

Lisa shrugged. "My lawyer works pro bono. He's swamped. He said because Andrew hadn't asked for joint custody when we divorced, the judge will see his motives and not grant it. I'm not so sure."

He leaned in closer to Lisa. "I'm sorry. I hope it works out."

She gave him a small smile. "Can I ask you about your house? Is that where your home gym was?"

"You remembered that? Yeah. I had a great home gym. And the house is beautiful. It was built in 1922 and has all the original woodwork, hardwood floors, and light fixtures. There's amazing stained and leaded glass windows and cool little nooks and cubbies. There's even a back servant's staircase from the kitchen to the upstairs, and servant quarters off the kitchen. It has a big yard, too. I just love that house."

"It sounds amazing. You should buy it back from her. I mean, if you can."

"That's the problem. I don't know if I can afford it now. My divorce was expensive. She not only got half my money and the house, but she gets thirty percent of royalties from any books I wrote while we were married. That's all my books up to this point. It cuts into my income quite a bit."

"Wow. I've never heard of that. That's terrible." Lisa looked appalled.

"I agree."

They threw away their garbage then continued their walk. Bailey was getting tired, so he didn't pull on the leash as much and Avery used that as an opportunity to praise and reward him for heeling. Soon, they'd made the complete circle and had crossed the street, heading home.

Avery stopped once more in front of his old house and stared up at it.

"You should call your ex and find out why she's selling it," Lisa suggested. "And you should try to get your dog back. Now that she's selling the house, she may not want Maddie anymore."

Avery thought about that a moment. Lisa was right. He should talk to Melissa. Maybe, after all these months, she'd at least give Maddie back. "I think you're right. I'm going to call her."

Lisa smiled. She took his free hand and held it and they began walking again toward home.

Avery liked how her hand felt in his. He'd been right. Today had turned out to be a good day after all.

* * *

Lisa couldn't believe she'd taken Avery's hand and held it all the way home. But it had seemed like such a natural thing to do. And she'd liked it. It felt good to hold someone's hand again. She wasn't sure what was going on between them and didn't want to analyze it. She just wanted to enjoy the warmth of her hand in his.

As they walked to her house, they passed Kristen and Ryan's home. Ryan was outside with little Marie, pulling her around in her wagon as Sam and Kristen watched from the porch.

"Hey, there," Ryan called, waving. "Nice day for a walk."

"It is," Lisa said. She went up their sidewalk with Avery and Bailey in tow. "What are you two up to?"

"We just got back from a walk around the block," Ryan said. "Now we're trying to figure out what to do for dinner."

"Where's Abby?" Kristen had come down from the porch with Sam at her heels. Sam and Bailey greeted each other. Bailey had known Sam since he was a small puppy and the two got along well.

"She's with Andrew this weekend," Lisa said. "Avery was teaching Bailey how to heel."

Ryan chuckled. "How did that go?"

"It's a process," Avery said with a grin.

"We were thinking of going to Gallagher's for dinner. Do you two want to join us? Mallory said she'd pack up Shannon and come along too," Kristen said.

Lisa eyed Avery to see his reaction. She wasn't sure if he was ready to join in on a crowd of neighbors and little children for dinner. He was great with Abby, but a table full of people might be too much for him. Especially after seeing his old house for sale today.

"I'm game if you are," Avery said after a moment.

"Are you sure?" she asked softly.

"Yeah. Why not?"

Lisa turned back to Kristen. "That sounds like fun. What time should we meet you there?"

The group planned to meet downtown at six. Since they were bringing their little ones, they had to be home early to get them to bed. Lisa told Avery she wanted to change before going, and he agreed he needed to clean up, too.

Lisa went inside and quickly fed Bailey his dinner. Then she cleaned up, combed out her hair, and added just a little more makeup. When she looked in her closet, she wondered what she should wear. A dress, even a casual one, might make it look like she was trying too hard. After all, this wasn't a date—it was a neighborhood get-together at a friend's pub. Yet, she wanted to look nice for Avery.

Wow. Just the thought that she wanted to look nice for a guy was big. Real big.

She decided on jeans again and a soft, lightweight blue sweater. She found a pair of western-style ankle boots in the back of her closet, and grinned. She'd bet that Avery would wear his cowboy boots, so he'd get a kick out of these. She slipped them on, then grabbed a light jacket for later.

She could hardly believe she was having dinner again tonight with Avery. But this time, her neighbors would be a buffer between them. Maybe that was a good thing. She'd felt they were growing closer as each day went by, and maybe they needed to take things slower. Really slow. But when she thought back to this afternoon, and how he'd casually wrapped his arm around her waist as they walked, and how she'd slipped her hand in his, sweet little chills ran through her. It had felt nice. All of it. The walking. Talking. Touching. Like it was the beginning of something.

I can't believe I'm thinking of the hermit this way.

Avery showed up at her door, also wearing jeans, a black shirt under a tan suede jacket, and his black cowboy boots. Lisa grinned.

"What are you smirking at?" he asked.

"I figured you'd wear your boots. See? I wore mine, too."

He smiled back. "They look nice. I'm glad I'm rubbing off on you."

It took twenty minutes to drive to the pub and another ten to find a parking space. Saturday night at Gallagher's was busy. Luckily, they knew the owner and he had a table in back set up for them with highchairs included.

Lisa and Avery were the last to arrive. They had saved two chairs for them at the end of the table. Mallory and James's little girl, Shannon, was nine months old and cute as a button. They had placed the highchairs next to each other to see how the children behaved together. So far, the girls were snacking on crackers and doing fine.

James had been bartending, and he came to the table to get their drink orders. He grinned at Avery and Lisa. "So, are you two an item?"

"James!" Mallory said, slapping his arm. "You don't ask people that."

Ryan laughed. "Yeah. But aren't we all thinking it?"

The women glared at their men, but Avery just laughed.

"Anything is possible," he said, smiling at Lisa.

Lisa's face grew warm and she quickly grabbed a menu to hide behind.

James joined them for dinner. Lisa was happy to see that Avery got along well with Ryan and James, and everyone accepted him as part of the group. He wasn't the cranky old hermit she'd thought he was. He'd just been burned so badly by his ex that he'd pulled away from society. She couldn't blame him. If she hadn't had Abby to keep up her spirits, she could have easily done the same thing after her divorce. But she was also lucky to have all these great friends.

After dinner, he drove her home and walked with her up to the porch. Like last night, they both stood there, suddenly acting awkward.

"I had a good time today," Avery said. "Sorry about the drama about my house. Otherwise, it was a nice walk."

"I had fun too. I'm glad we went to dinner with everyone. They're a great group," Lisa said.

"They are." He drew closer and his eyes sparkled mischievously. "So. Are we an item?"

His question took her by surprise, as everything he'd done had. "Um. I'm not sure. Maybe?"

Avery leaned down and gently brushed his lips over hers. When she didn't protest, he slid his arms around her waist and pulled her to him. Lisa liked how his arms felt around her. Just as he was about to kiss her, Bailey started barking from inside the house.

Lisa pulled back and laughed. So did Avery.

"Well, I guess we'll never know if we're an item," he said.

She grinned. "We'll see."

Avery laughed again, gave her a small wave, and headed to his car.

Chapter Ten

Avery sat at his computer, still feeling warm inside from holding Lisa's body close to his. The slight brush of his lips against hers had been sweet. Unfortunately, he hadn't been able to go farther before Bailey shook off the mood.

Well, hopefully they'd get another chance—soon.

He'd had a wonderful time today despite seeing his old house for sale. A week ago, in his angry state of mind, that would have put him over the edge. But since meeting Lisa—well, meeting her properly—his anger had mostly abated. Mostly. He still had a bone to pick with his ex-wife. And today, as he'd walked along with Lisa and Bailey, he'd made a decision: he was going to insist Melissa give Maddie back. It was time he stopped brooding and wallowing and started standing up for himself again. And it was time to bring Maddie home.

He looked at the Word file in front of him and read the last few lines. He liked these new characters. They had great potential. After getting back into the story, his fingers flew over the keyboard. He'd found his voice again, because he'd found his muse. Lisa had brought the feel of romance back into his life, and that made writing about it so much easier.

He smiled at the thought of the word "romance" connected

to Lisa. He'd like to romance her. She deserved to be romanced, and he was going to make sure she was.

The next morning, Avery left the house early and stopped at a florist shop to buy roses for Lisa. He looked at the red ones, but they didn't seem right. Pink? No. White roses? He didn't think so. When he saw the yellow roses, he smiled. Yes. Lisa would like yellow roses. At least, he hoped she would.

It was nearly noon when he walked across the street to bring her the roses. He was officially going to ask her out on a proper date, not just a casual dinner. He wanted to make his serious intentions known. If the entire neighborhood saw him going to her house with roses, he didn't mind. He was falling fast for Lisa, and he didn't care who knew.

She opened the door, a surprised look on her face. Her hair had been hastily put up and she was wearing shorts and a sweat-shirt. Avery thought she looked adorable.

"Avery. Hi. I wasn't expecting you." She swiped her hand over her hair to smooth it but to no avail.

He handed her the roses. "I know. But I had to see you. These are for you."

"They're beautiful." She looked stunned that he'd brought her flowers. "How did you know I liked yellow roses?"

He smiled. "I just thought you would. Can I come in?"

"Sure. I was picking up the house and doing laundry. Be careful where you step. I'm going to get a vase." She turned and headed for the kitchen and he followed her.

"Where's Bailey? I'm usually tripping over him," Avery asked.

"He's in the backyard. Don't worry, as soon as he senses you're here, he'll come running." She reached up high in a cabi-net and pulled down a glass vase. Turning, she smiled at him. "So, what did I do to deserve such beautiful flowers?"

Avery drew closer and gazed into her eyes. "I want to do this right. I'm officially declaring my intentions to you."

Her brows rose. "Intentions? My, that is serious."

"I am serious. I want you to know you mean more to me than just the neighbor across the street with the runaway dog. I'd like to ask you out on an official date, not just a casual get-together. I want to romance you, woo you, and see where it goes. With your permission."

She laughed nervously. "Are you being serious or just kidding me? Because no one has ever asked my permission to date me before, let alone woo me."

"I'm being serious." He put his arms around her and kissed her sweetly on the tip of her nose. Just a nice, soft kiss. "I want to do this right, because you deserve to be treated right."

Tears filled Lisa's eyes. "That's so sweet."

"Don't cry," he said, panicking. "I didn't mean to make you cry."

She laughed. "They're happy tears." She brushed away the tears and smiled up at him.

"Does this mean you'll go on an official date with me? We'll dress up like adults, eat at a nice restaurant, not a pub, and I'll wine and dine you."

"Yes," she said, smiling widely. "I'd love to do that."

Just as their lips touched, the doorbell rang. Bailey came sprinting past them, barking loudly.

"That's Andrew bringing Abby home." Lisa rushed behind the dog to the door and opened it. Avery followed her to the living room but stayed a distance away.

"Mommy!" Abby called as Andrew carried her inside. "Baywee!"

Lisa took Abby into her arms and held her close. "I missed you, you little monkey," she said, cuddling the little girl.

"Get down, you mutt!" Andrew yelled, pushing Bailey off of him. "Stupid dog."

"He's just excited to see Abby." Lisa rolled her eyes. She put her hand down, palm flat, and Bailey stopped jumping and sat.

"Good job," Avery said, impressed.

Andrew glared at Avery. "Why's the gardener still here?" he asked, addressing Lisa.

"He's not the gardener. He's my neighbor." She set Abby down and the little girl ran to Bailey and wrapped her arms around him. He let her, as he always did, sitting patiently.

"How did it go with Abby?" Lisa asked Andrew.

"It was fine, just like I said it would be. She stopped crying as soon as I pulled away from the house. She always does. You just worry too much."

Avery noticed that Lisa's face tightened. Andrew talked down to her. It was so obvious he thought he was superior to her. Andrew definitely thought he was better than him, too. But he noticed she didn't say anything back.

"Has she had lunch yet?" Lisa asked.

"No. I figured you could take care of that. Katrina was in a rush to meet friends for lunch, so that's where we're headed."

Yeah. The girlfriend is way more important than your daughter, Avery thought.

Andrew stood there a moment and looked Avery's way again. "So, are you two dating or something?"

Lisa frowned. "Is it your business? Maybe you should get going so you can feed Katrina."

Avery grinned. *Chalk one up for Lisa!*

"Fine. Be that way. See you in a couple of weeks," Andrew said. He turned and stalked off the porch without even saying goodbye to Abby.

Lisa shut the door, turned to Avery, and shook her head. Avery noticed she refrained from saying anything negative about her ex in front of Abby. He liked that about her. She was genuinely nice.

"Come on, munchkin," Lisa said, scooping up Abby as the little girl giggled. "How do chicken nuggets and carrots sound for lunch?" She turned to Avery. "Want to stay?"

"Sure. I like chicken nuggets." He grinned.

She laughed. "I'll make us sandwiches. Grown-up food."

Avery followed them into the kitchen, happy he felt like he belonged here.

* * *

Monday morning Avery called Melissa to see if they could meet somewhere.

"Why?" she asked, sounding suspicious.

"I just want to talk. There's still some things we haven't completely ironed out," Avery said.

"The divorce has been final for months. There's nothing else to talk about," she insisted.

He took a breath to stay calm. "Just meet me, okay? How about Gallagher's at noon? We can have lunch."

"Well, okay. As long as you're paying," she said.

"Don't I always?" he grumbled.

Avery arrived a few minutes before noon. James was behind the bar, so he stopped to say hello.

"Back so soon?" James asked. "You must love my food."

"Actually, I do. Best burgers in town. But I'm also meeting my ex-wife," Avery told him. He knew if he didn't say it up front, rumors might spread around the neighborhood. "We have to discuss a few unfinished details."

"That sounds like fun." James grimaced. "Beer or something harder?"

Avery laughed. "Just a Coke. I need to keep my wits about me." He found a table in the back, and waited for Melissa.

She arrived ten minutes late—typical—and sauntered in wearing a tight, short black skirt and a blue, silky blouse that showed off her perfect curves. Her heels clicked on the wood floor and every man in the bar turned and stared at her long, shapely legs—and God knows what else—as she made her way to Avery's table. At one time, he would have puffed up with pride because this gorgeous woman was with him. But not today. He knew her both inside and out, and she no longer looked beautiful in his eyes.

Melissa sat down across from Avery, crossed her legs, and asked in her smooth voice, "So what is it you want?"

"Why don't we order first, then we can talk," he suggested. James had approached the table with menus and Melissa smiled up at him and ordered a white wine.

As they looked through the menu, she gave Avery a quick, appraising look. "You don't look as bad as the last time I saw you. Looks like you've finally shaved and had your hair cut."

"Gee. Thanks."

She shrugged. "Well, you looked like a homeless man for a while."

"I was a homeless man for a while. Remember? You took the house and I had to live in a hotel until I found a place to live. I basically bought the first house I looked at."

She laughed softly. "If you can call that a house. It's more like a shack. You could have bought something better than that."

Avery tried hard not to glare at her. He had to remember

why he was here. If he wanted Maddie back, he had to play nice. "It suits me fine. It's a roof over my head."

James came back and took their food order. Avery noticed that Melissa flirted shamelessly with James, but he seemed to just let it roll off his back. Avery suspected that James got that all the time from pretty women and knew how to ignore it while being polite.

Once James was gone, Melissa's flirty smile faded.

"I walked by the house on Saturday. You put it up for sale. Why?" Avery asked.

"It's my house. I can do whatever I want with it," she said.

"Yeah, but you insisted on getting it in the divorce settlement. You said you loved that house and wanted to live there. So, what changed?"

"I don't want it anymore. Ross has a gorgeous house up in White Bear Lake and we've decided to make that our main residence. He also has a huge townhouse in Chanhassen if we want to stay in town. So, we don't need my house anymore." She glanced around, looking bored.

Avery's could feel his blood pressure rising. "What did you do with all the furniture inside our house? Did you sell it?"

Melissa rolled her eyes and sighed. "*My* house. Not *our* house. What do you care? You got everything out of there that you wanted."

"Not everything. What about the workout equipment? And the stereo equipment? What about the huge television in the exercise room?"

"It's all going with the house." She waved her perfectly manicured hand through the air as if to brush it all away. "I don't need any of that stuff anymore."

Avery sat back in his seat, trying hard not to blow up. He'd wanted to keep his house. He'd wanted to keep everything in it. He couldn't believe she was just tossing it all aside and was going to profit off the house he'd bought with his money.

"Stop glaring at me," she said. "It's mine to sell. If you want all that stuff and the house, then buy it back."

Avery leaned on the table, closer to her. "I already bought it once. I shouldn't have to buy it again. Besides, I can't afford that house since you got half my savings and thirty percent of my royalties on every book I've written since we were married. Between you, my publisher, and my agent each taking a cut, that doesn't leave me with much, now does it?"

She flipped her hair back and said haughtily, "That's your problem, not mine."

A waitress approached their table and delivered their food. Melissa ordered another glass of wine before the waitress left. Avery stared down at his food, no longer hungry. He was too angry to eat. Apparently, their conversation hadn't affected Melissa. She began eating her salad.

"Aren't you going to eat?" she asked. "Or did you invite me here just to harass me?"

Avery pushed his plate aside. "I invited you here to ask you for only one thing. One thing that I know you don't care about and couldn't possibly want. I'd like to have Maddie back."

One perfect brow rose. "So, that's what you want? The dog?" She shook her head. "I swear, I think you loved that dog more than you ever loved me."

You've got that right, he wanted to say but held it in. "None of that matters now. You got everything else you wanted. You know you only kept Maddie because you knew I wanted her. I'd like her back. Please."

Melissa laughed. "Now you say please?"

"You can't possibly want to keep her. You never even liked her when we were together." He was growing desperate.

Melissa assessed him a moment, then turned her glossy lips into a smile. "I've been thinking that thirty percent of your royalties isn't enough. I had a terrible lawyer. Maybe if I had forty percent, you and I could make a deal."

Avery felt as if he'd been smacked by a truck. "You're blackmailing me?"

"Of course not. I'm just trying to make a deal that suits both of us."

"No. Absolutely not! I won't give you another penny of my money."

She sneered at him. "Well, too bad then. I've taken a liking to Maddie and she adores me. She also loves Ross. You can't have her back."

Avery curled his hands into fists. "You're an evil bitch, you know that?"

"And you're a boring, washed-up writer who only cares about himself. So, enjoy your little shack house without your dog while I live the good life with Ross, who, by the way, knows how to make me happy."

Heart pounding, Avery pulled out his wallet, dropped a fifty on the table, and stood. "Enjoy your lunch, Cruella. The next time you hear from me will be through my lawyer, suing you for custody of my dog." He walked away quickly, but not fast enough to outrun her laughter before he made it out the door.

Chapter Eleven

Lisa was beat by the time she came home late Monday afternoon. Several children in school had been sent home with fevers and many were already absent with colds and the flu. When she picked Abby up from day care, the little girl was sniffling. Lisa was worried that Abby might get sick too, and then what would she do? The school only allowed five personal days a year for a sick child, unless it was a major illness; after that, she could use her own sick leave. Lisa couldn't afford to miss work without pay, so she silently prayed that all Abby had was a runny nose.

She changed into comfy clothes and gave Abby a snack. Then she set Abby on the living room floor to play with Bailey. As Lisa was wondering what to make for dinner, she walked over to the picture window and stared across the street at Avery's house. There was a light on in his front bedroom, but that was all she saw. She supposed he was working and didn't want to bother him, but she really wanted to invite him over for dinner.

After less than a week it felt strange not to have him here.

She decided to call and ask him how his day was. She hoped he'd had a better one than hers. He answered on the third ring. "Hey there."

She smiled. She liked how in such a short time his voice

sounded comforting to her. "Hi. I was just going to ask how your day was. Hopefully better than mine."

"I've had better," he said gruffly.

Lisa hesitated. She'd obviously interrupted him. "Would it help to talk about it or would you rather not?" she asked.

There was a long pause that made her nervous. Was she butting in where she didn't belong? She'd thought they were at a point in their friendship where she could call for no reason, but maybe not. Yet, hadn't he asked for permission to romance her? She began second-guessing everything until he answered.

"I'd rather hear about your day," he said in a friendlier tone. "Are you okay?"

She sighed so loudly with relief that it made Avery laugh.

"That bad, huh?"

"Yes and no. It's the fourth week of school and kids are passing around all kinds of illnesses. It's to be expected, but it's worrisome. Now Abby has the sniffles and I'm scared she'll get sick too."

"Maybe she just has allergies. The leaves are turning, and the weather is cooling down. It could be something as simple as that," he suggested.

"I know. I'm just around sick kids all day so I worry. What about you? Did you go walking with Bailey today?"

"No. Not today. I may tomorrow, though. To be honest, I met up with my ex, Melissa, for lunch and asked for Maddie back."

Now she understood why he sounded like his old hermit self when he'd answered the phone. "What happened?"

"She said no. And she flaunted the fact that she's selling the house with everything in it. Everything! She said a few other things that made me mad, but I won't bother you with those.

It doesn't matter anyway. I can't do anything about the house being sold or about Maddie. But I did, stupidly, threaten to sue her for my dog. She only laughed at me."

Lisa's heart went out to Avery. He didn't deserve the way his ex treated him. "Do you want to come over for dinner and we can talk?" she asked. She wasn't sure what she'd make, but she could figure out something. "It sounds like you could use a friend to rant to."

"Thanks, but I think I'd be terrible company. It would be better if I stayed home and kept writing."

Something about the tone of his voice made Lisa sad. "Avery? You're not going back into your dark little hermit cave, are you? You were having such a good time with the rest of us out here in the world."

He chuckled. "Honestly, I do want to crawl back into my dark space, but I'll try not to. I'll take a raincheck on that dinner, and I'll take Bailey out for a long walk tomorrow."

"Okay."

"Oh, and does Friday night at six sound good to you?" he asked.

"For what?"

"For our first official date. Remember? I'm trying to romance you." His voice sounded lighter than it had earlier.

"Sure. That sounds fine. I'll see if Kristen can babysit."

"Great. Wear something dressy. I'm going to wine and dine you."

She laughed. "This should be interesting."

"And tell Abby I said hi. I'm sure I'll see her tomorrow," he said.

"I will. Happy writing."

"Thanks. I need all the good karma I can get."

Lisa hung up, thinking about Friday night. Dressy. What was she going to wear that was dressy? She hadn't dressed up for a dinner date in years.

The rest of the week, Abby's sniffles continued but except for a little sneezing, she seemed fine. She had a good appetite and was playing normally. Lisa figured Avery was right—she probably had allergies.

Kristen agreed to babysit Abby on Friday night, and when she heard that Lisa needed a nice dress, she invited her over to dig through her closet.

"I have a bunch of fancy dresses," she told her. "I used to go to formal dinners and parties with the surgeon I was dating before I met Ryan. I'm sure there's one in the bunch that would fit you."

Lisa had a ball going through Kristen's dresses and little Abby and Marie also played dress-up with some old beads and hats that Kristen had found in the back of the closet. After trying a few dresses on, Lisa settled on a royal blue sheath that accented her long waist and brought out the color of her eyes.

"That dress never fit me right," Kristen said. "And now I know why. It was made for you."

Lisa loved how the dress felt on her, how it shimmered as she moved in the light. It was sleeveless, so they dug through the closet some more and came up with a black, bolero sweater that had silver threading through it that made it sparkle. "I have black pumps at home that will work well with this," Lisa said.

After changing back into her jeans and sweater, Lisa hugged Kristen. "Thanks so much for letting me borrow this. And for babysitting. I haven't done anything like this in a long time."

"Borrow it? The way that dress looks on you, it's yours. I'll never wear it. Maybe you'll get some use out of it," Kristen said.

"And you're welcome. I'm always happy to help a budding love affair."

"Love affair?" Lisa laughed. "I'm not sure about that."

"I am," Kristen said with a wink. "Avery turned out not to be so bad after all. And now he's going to wine and dine you? You don't find men like that every day."

Lisa had to agree with Kristen. Avery was unique. She was excited, and a little anxious about officially going out with him. She hadn't been with a man other than Andrew in years. And she hadn't exactly been a player before meeting her ex-husband. As much as she wanted to get to know Avery better, there was a little bit of trepidation there too.

Avery had avoided her again on Tuesday, although he'd called and said he'd walked Bailey that day and they'd had a good time. He'd told her he was still trying to get past his nasty conversation with Melissa but promised he was staying out of the dark place. On Wednesday, he came over to see her and they ordered pizza to be delivered. He stayed a while after dinner then left before she put Abby down for bed.

"Are you sure you're okay?" she asked him as they stood at the door.

He leaned over and kissed her sweetly on the cheek. "I'm fine. I'm just trying to figure out how to get my dog back. Don't worry. I'll be my charming self by Friday."

Lisa waved goodbye as he walked across the street. She wished she could do something to help him get Maddie back. But there was nothing she could do.

Thursday night, Abby was crabby and didn't want to eat much or play with Bailey. She felt warm to the touch, and the thermometer showed her temperature as 102 degrees. Lisa gave her a dose of children's Tylenol and her fever went down. By

Friday morning, she seemed fine again, so Lisa brought her in to the day care.

That evening, Lisa was more careful than usual applying her makeup and styling her hair. Her blond hair was naturally straight, so she used a curling iron to add some waves and let it hang down her back. Then came the dress, the sweater, and her heels.

"Mama pretty," Abby said from the middle of the bed where she'd been playing. So far, her fever hadn't returned, and she seemed fine. Lisa gave her a hug. "I hope Avery will think that, too," she said.

Five minutes to six, Kristen showed up. "You look great! Avery's going to be blown away."

Lisa felt a blush rise to her cheeks. She wasn't used to this type of attention. "Thanks. And thanks again for watching Abby. She's eaten dinner already and can have a snack before bed. She usually goes down by seven."

"Sounds good." Kristen lifted Abby from the bed and twirled her around. "We're going to have fun, aren't we?"

Lisa watched her as she made Abby giggle. Kristen was four months pregnant, yet only had a slight bump that you wouldn't even notice if you didn't know. She was thankful for neighbors like Kristen and Ryan. She didn't know what she'd have done after Andrew left her if she hadn't had the support of the many women in the neighborhood.

Right at six, the doorbell rang. Bailey was at the door first, and Lisa had to move him away before answering it. "Hi."

Avery's eyes lit up when he saw her. "Hi, yourself. You look gorgeous."

"Thanks." She nervously ran her hand over her dress to smooth non-existent wrinkles. She didn't understand why she felt jittery. It was just Avery after all. He was wearing a blue-gray suit with a tie and looked like a completely different guy. "You look nice too."

He grinned. "Well. As good as a hermit can look."

"You two go along and have fun," Kristen said from behind them. "Don't waste your time together standing in the doorway."

Lisa and Avery both laughed. She picked up her purse from the table in the entryway and waved goodbye to Abby and Kristen, then they were off.

Avery drove on the highway toward town. She caught him glancing over at her, which made her self-conscious.

"You do look incredible," he said. "Is that a new dress?"

"No. Not on my budget, unfortunately. Kristen loaned it to me. I guess she used to have a pretty active social life before she met Ryan."

"Really?" He looked surprised. "I mean, she's a pretty woman and all, but I got the impression she was more into her career as a nurse than socializing."

"I think she was serious about her work. But she dated an older guy who was very social and then she met Ryan and they clicked. She loved working but she loves being home with Marie, too. And soon, she'll have another little one to take care of."

"She's expecting?" Avery asked.

"Yeah."

"Wow. I didn't know. Good for them."

Lisa studied Avery. He was so good with Abby, she wondered if he'd ever wanted children. "Did you and Melissa ever talk about having kids?"

"God, no," he said quickly. "I wouldn't have minded having one or two children, but it would never have even crossed Melissa's mind. So, we didn't discuss it."

"Oh." Lisa decided she should change the subject. Technically, this was their first real date and asking about children probably wasn't a smart idea. Avery might get a sense she was already feeling him out as husband material.

Which was amusing because the last thing she needed was a husband.

They arrived downtown and Avery pulled up to a very expensive hotel that had valet parking. "There's a wonderful restaurant on the top floor with a beautiful view of the city," Avery said. He got out and ran around to open her door, then helped her out of the car. The valet took the keys, gave him a ticket, and drove off.

Avery and Lisa walked inside the hotel. The lobby was decorated in a very modern style with shiny silver, mirrors, and a waterfall on one wall. Going directly to the elevators, he pushed the number fifteen, and up they went.

Lisa stood in the elevator, unsure of what to say. It was funny. When they were in jeans and T-shirts eating pizza at her table, the conversation flowed easily. But now, dressed up and going to an expensive restaurant, it felt like any familiarity had disappeared.

The elevator stopped and the doors opened. Spread out in front of her was a huge restaurant seemingly made of glass. Beyond, she saw Minneapolis's skyscape. Her eyes widened in awe.

"Gorgeous, isn't it?" Avery whispered, his breath tickling her ear. "Wait until sunset."

The hostess, in a sleek, black dress, stood at a glass podium a few steps from the elevator. She checked off his name and said they would come get him when their table was ready. She showed them to a table in the bar where they could wait, then left.

"I'm impressed already," Lisa said, sitting close to him at the small table.

"Wait until you sit by the window. It's amazing. And the food is incredible."

A waiter took their drink order. Lisa ordered wine and Avery had a scotch and soda. As they waited for their drinks, Lisa shifted in her seat. This was beyond any place she'd ever been to. Andrew liked to eat at nice places for special occasions, but nothing had ever compared to this.

"How did you find this restaurant?" she asked.

"My agent brought me here the one and only time he came to see me. He stayed at this hotel. I have to admit I was blown away. So, I saved coming back for a very special occasion." His eyes twinkled.

"This is the first time you've been back?" This surprised her. She figured he must have always come to places like this. He seemed comfortable here.

"Yes. It was the first place I thought of when I asked you out. I wanted our first date to be perfect."

The waiter brought their drinks. Avery lifted his glass. "To first dates."

"To first dates," she repeated and clinked her glass to his. After taking a sip, she gazed at him and shook her head.

"What?" he looked concerned.

"When you say you're going to wine and dine a woman, you really mean it."

A warm chuckle erupted from Avery. "You deserve the very best. So just relax and enjoy." He moved in closer to her. "I know I'm going to enjoy tonight."

A sweet chill ran through her. Avery was so handsome tonight, so absolutely sexy. She hadn't thought this way about a man in so long that it surprised her. But it was a nice surprise.

They were shown to their table which was right next to one

of the large, floor-to-ceiling windows that allowed a generous view. The sun was just setting, painting the city in a red and orange glaze. The Mississippi River in the distance sparkled in the fading light, and soon the lights on bridges and buildings began to glow. It was spectacular, and Lisa watched in complete amazement.

"Not a bad choice for a hermit, huh?" Avery said, a mischievous grin on his face.

"No. Not bad at all."

The menus showed no prices for meals. She knew only the most expensive restaurants did that. Obviously, Avery must be able to afford such a place, but it still made her nervous. Avery must have seen her apprehension about the menu because he reached over and placed his hand over hers.

"Order anything you'd like. Please. This is a special night. Anything goes."

She smiled and nodded, enjoying the feel of his hand over hers.

They ordered dinner—he ordered the steak and lobster and she decided on chicken Kiev. Avery moved his chair closer to hers and held her hand as they stared out at the darkening skyline, the lights twinkling like diamonds in the sky. It felt magical. Enchanting.

"You know, you could have taken me to Red Lobster, and I would have thought that was extravagant," she said, grinning.

Avery laughed. "I'll remember that next time. But for now, this will have to do."

"It will more than just 'do,'" she said. "It's amazing. Thank you."

He leaned toward her and kissed her lightly on the cheek. "You deserve it. Enjoy."

She knew the real Avery was just as content with pizza and beer. But this was the first time she'd seen the successful side of Avery. The bestselling author who lived in a mansion across from Lake Harriet and who was used to having his own in-house gym. He probably had a pool, too, and she knew he'd traveled on expensive vacations without even blinking about the price. But from what she could see, both sides of him were the same. He was still the guy who teased her, who'd dug up her yard to fix her fence, and who'd offered to take her dog on walks. She liked that Avery, and this one.

Their food came. Lisa's meal melted in her mouth; it was that delicious. Avery had switched from alcohol to water, and again, she was thankful for that. They talked about things other than their work or her everyday life. Instead, Avery asked her about places she'd been or would like to travel to. He told her about trips he'd taken, and places he still wanted to see.

"If I could take a year off and travel around the world, I would," he said. "By plane, ship, and train. Something different for a change."

"I've always wanted to take a ship from New York to England," Lisa confessed. "A fancy ship, like the Titanic, except one that wouldn't sink."

He laughed. "Yes. Not sinking is a must. It sounds amazing, but what makes you want to do that?"

"My great-grandparents came over from England on a ship. I'm sure it wasn't luxurious for them, because they were poor. But I always thought it would be wonderful to stand on the deck and see the ocean all around. An adventure."

They sat there in a little bubble of their own making, unaware of anyone else around them as they told each other their dreams and goals. Avery had led an interesting life already, and still had so much more he wanted to do. Lisa hadn't been as fortunate but dreamed of a time when she could also do things she'd always hoped to.

Their plates were taken away and a plate of chocolate cheese-cake with strawberries on top, and two forks, was set on the table between them.

"I'm so full, I'm not sure I could eat another bite," Lisa said. But Avery coaxed her to try it, and when she did, she sighed.

"It's heavenly, right?" he asked.

"It's perfect." She said it as she gazed into those amazing dark blue eyes of his. "It's all perfect."

Lisa heard her phone buzz from inside her small purse. She thought of ignoring it, then realized it might be Kristen. She looked up at Avery. "I should answer that."

"Go ahead. I'll take care of the bill while you do." He left the table.

Lisa pulled out her phone and saw it was, indeed, Kristen. "Hi. Is everything okay?"

"I'm sorry to bother you on your date," she said, sounding harried. "But Abby isn't doing very well. She went to bed just fine, but then woke up crying and feverish. Then she threw up. I thought she'd be okay after that, but she's still quite warm and too upset to even try to sleep."

"Oh no." Lisa could hear Abby crying in the background and her heart went out to her baby. "She was like that last night, without the vomiting. Did you take her temperature?"

"Yes. It's a hundred and two, so not dangerous but not good either. I hesitated about giving her Tylenol because of her upset stomach."

"Yeah, I would have done the same. We just finished dinner, so I'll come home. I'm so sorry about this. I thought she was feeling better."

"I'm the one who's sorry. But I knew you'd be upset if I didn't tell you she wasn't feeling well," Kristen said. "Don't rush. I'm keeping an eye on her."

"We'll be there in a bit. Thanks, Kristen."

Avery returned to the table. "Is something wrong?"

"I have to go home. I'm so sorry. Abby is sick. She's been fighting something all week and it's worse tonight."

"Don't be sorry. Of course you have to go home. We can do this another night."

They went downstairs and the valet retrieved his car. Soon, they were on the highway heading back to the neighborhood.

"I feel so bad. I shouldn't have left Abby tonight. I just didn't think she was that sick. Poor Kristen. I hope she doesn't get what Abby has." She felt terrible. Thinking of her baby being sick and not being there broke her heart.

"Don't blame yourself," Avery said soothingly. "I'm sure Abby will be fine. Kristen is a nurse, too. She's the best person, other than you, to take care of Abby."

"I know. But it's hard. I'm always there for her, and the one night I'm not, she's sick."

Avery reached across the console and took her hand in his. "Don't beat yourself up. No going to the dark place, okay?" He turned and smiled at her.

He was right. She'd be home soon enough, and Abby would probably already be sleeping. "Okay." She squeezed his hand. "Thank you."

"For what?"

"For the wonderful night. For the amazing meal. And for understanding I had to cut the date short. I appreciate it all."

"Only a jerk wouldn't understand," he said. "It's Abby. She's the best part of your life. I know that. And I don't want anything to happen to her, either."

A lump formed in Lisa's throat as she forced back tears. Avery couldn't have said anything more heartwarming. The fact that he understood how important her daughter was to her, and he accepted it, was better than a hundred romantic dates.

She knew right then that he was a keeper.

Chapter Twelve

Avery sat at his computer later that night, trying to concentrate on his characters but instead could only think of the real people in his life. He felt terrible for Lisa. She'd looked so stricken when she'd told him that Abby was sick and she had to go home. She'd actually paled, and for a moment, he thought something worse had happened to the little girl. Still, any sickness in a child that young was scary, and he hadn't hesitated for a second when Lisa had asked to leave.

They'd had such a wonderful time up to that point, though. He was happy he'd taken her there, even though it had been excessive. Lisa didn't get to enjoy luxury like that. Her life was endless work, between her job and caring for Abby. And although he knew that she adored Abby—he did too—it was fun to give her a little time off from reality. But then, when they'd walked into Lisa's house and poor little Abby was red-faced from crying, reality came charging back to her.

After Kristen had left—telling Lisa not to hesitate to call her if Abby grew worse—Avery had offered to stay a while and do whatever he could. But Lisa, looking frazzled, had told him to go ahead home. She needed to calm Abby down and watch over her to make sure her fever didn't rise. Lisa said she'd call him in the morning and let him know how Abby was doing.

Avery had felt so helpless and useless. He'd gone home like she'd asked but wished there'd been more he could have done.

Now he sat here, feeling even more incompetent as the characters wouldn't do what he wanted them to. Again, the story was plodding along, and he couldn't seem to straighten it out. Worse yet, his career was riding on this book. He'd been given the extension, but they expected a bestseller after waiting so long. If he didn't hand in the best book of his career, it would be over. No more contracts. No more money.

Just as he'd thought his life was coming together, it seemed to be falling apart again. The stress of that wasn't helping matters at all.

Avery looked out his window and saw that Lisa's lights were still on. Abby hadn't gone to sleep yet, which meant that Lisa hadn't either. His heart went out to her. She was such a wonderful, loving, caring mother. She was always thinking of Abby, putting the little girl ahead of herself and her own needs. He found that heartwarming and admired her dedication. Lisa was more than a beautiful woman. She had a good heart and a kind soul; two things he hadn't experienced from the women he'd been with before, especially Melissa. If he were fortunate enough to win Lisa's heart, he'd feel like the richest man on earth.

He'd never felt this way about any other woman in his life.

Maybe that was what was missing from his novel. That kind of dedication. That kind of love.

Turning back to his screen, he began typing again, determined to make this the best story he'd ever written.

* * *

Avery awoke late the next day after staying up until three in the morning, writing. He showered and dressed, then called Lisa, hoping he wasn't waking her. She answered on the first ring.

"Hi."

"Hi. How's Abby feeling?" he asked.

"She's doing better, I think," Lisa said, sounding tired. "She didn't sleep much last night, then this morning, finally fell to sleep. Her fever is down. I'm going to try to get her to drink more fluids today and hopefully she'll feel better."

"Do you need anything? I'd be happy to help. I'm great at moral support."

"Thanks, but I don't need anything. I'm wiped out. I'm going to try to get some sleep while she naps and just see how things go."

"Okay," Avery said, disappointed he couldn't be of any help. "I'll be here if you need me."

"Thanks. And thanks for last night. I'm sorry it ended so abruptly. I had a wonderful time while it lasted."

"Me too. We'll do it again. Maybe we'll go to Red Lobster next time." He chuckled.

She laughed. "That's fine with me."

"If I go for a walk later today, do you mind if I bring Bailey? I'll be quiet when I get him."

"That would be great," she said. "He could use a break. He's been lying beside Abby all night, a worried look on his face. Poor puppy. He doesn't understand why she's so upset."

"Doesn't surprise me," he said. "He's totally devoted to her."

After they hung up, Avery was restless. He wanted to be there for Lisa, but he also understood that there was nothing he could do.

Around eleven, Avery checked Lisa's backyard and saw Bailey

there. He'd brought his own leash for the dog, so using the gate key that he still had, he clipped it on Bailey's collar, locked the gate, and headed out for a walk. As he passed the hole in the tall bushes between Lisa and Kristen's houses, he saw Kristen coming outside, waving at him.

"Have you talked to Lisa?" she asked, sounding concerned.

"I did earlier, but she said she was going to try to take a nap. She said Abby's fever was down and she'd finally fallen asleep."

"Oh, good." Kristen looked relieved. "I didn't want to bother her in case she was sleeping. I'm glad to hear that Abby's feeling better."

"Yeah. Lisa was upset last night. I'm glad you were the one babysitting. She trusts you completely with Abby."

"I adore Lisa and Abby. I'm glad I was there too." She glanced down at Bailey. "He was with Abby the whole time last night. Wouldn't leave her side. I'm glad you're taking him for a walk. The poor boy needs a distraction."

Avery said goodbye and took off. He walked in the same direction as he and Lisa had gone the weekend before. It seemed like a lifetime ago that they had walked to the park together, yet it had only been a week. He worked with Bailey, keeping the dog close to his left side and encouraging him not to pull on the leash. Avery stopped a few times on purpose, saying "Stop," then "Heel" when he started again. He knew it would take some time before Bailey caught on, but he wanted to get him started anyway.

As Avery passed his previous house across from Lake Harriet, he paused a moment, staring up at it. He had really loved that house. He wished he was able to buy it back but wasn't sure if he could swing it. Especially now that Melissa had threatened to sue him for a higher percentage of income. But if he could write a great book for his publisher, maybe they'd renew his contract and he could afford this house again. He sighed. That was a lot of maybes.

When he brought Bailey back to the yard, Lisa poked her head out the back door.

"Thanks for walking Bailey. I'll bet he had a good time."

Avery thought she still looked tired. Never having had a child of his own, he hadn't realized how stressful it was to take care of a sick little girl. His respect for Lisa was growing by the minute. "I was happy to do it. He did have fun. Is there anything I can do for you? Would you like me to bring over dinner later?"

"Thanks, but we're just going to eat the chicken noodle soup that Kristen brought today, and crackers. I'm hoping Abby can keep that down."

"Okay." He was disappointed, but he understood. He didn't want to barge in when she was busy with Abby. "Let me know if you need anything. I'll be at my desk, trying to write."

She smiled. "Trying to write?"

"It doesn't always come easy."

This made her smile wider. He liked making her smile.

She called Bailey inside and waved to Avery before closing the door.

As he made his way home, he wondered what he'd eat for dinner. Did it matter? For some reason, dinner tasted better when he shared it with Lisa and Abby.

Boy had his life changed in such a short time.

* * *

Lisa had been doing whatever she could to keep Abby's fever down all day and into the evening. She'd placed a cool washcloth around the little girl's neck and on her forehead. She'd given her a soothing bath. Even after giving her baby Tylenol, her fever hovered between 102 and 103. As a nurse, Lisa knew that she shouldn't worry unless the fever spiked up to 104, but as a mother, she was growing frantic. Abby hadn't been able to keep fluids down for very long each time she drank, and she was growing listless. A toddler who didn't want to play or run around was a sick child. Even Bailey couldn't bring out any excitement in Abby.

As the evening wore on, Lisa grew more concerned.

She called Kristen to ask her advice and she said the same thing that Lisa already knew. But Kristen told her to follow her instincts. "If you're really worried, take her to the emergency room. Better safe than sorry."

Lisa agreed. But it seemed silly to bring her in just to be told she should go home.

Throughout the evening, she'd tried calling Andrew to let him know that Abby was sick. She knew there was nothing he could do, but as Abby's father, he should know what was happening. It annoyed her at first that he didn't answer his phone, then her annoyance turned into anger. He should at least listen to his voice mail when it was about his daughter. This just emphasized what a selfish person he could be.

Abby's fever had gone down a little by the time Lisa put her to bed. She fell asleep and Lisa kept the baby monitor by her side as she tried to sleep on the sofa. Lisa hoped it was a good sign that her fever had dropped. Looking exhausted too, Bailey curled up in front of Abby's door and slept.

Abby awoke an hour later, crying. Lisa was up immediately and went to get her. When she picked her up, the toddler felt hot—too hot. Lisa's heart pounded. This wasn't normal. She couldn't wait this out another moment. Lisa wrapped a blanket around Abby, grabbed her purse and car keys, and ran out of the house.

She was just finishing buckling Abby into her car seat when Avery came racing across the street with a flashlight.

"Is she worse?"

Lisa looked up at him and saw his face was creased with concern. "Yes. I'm taking her to the emergency room."

"I'll drive," he said. "You can sit in back with Abby and keep her calm."

Lisa didn't argue. She was actually relieved she didn't have to drive.

"Which hospital?" Avery wanted to know.

"Children's Hospital is the closest. I'll give you the directions." Lisa pulled out her phone and told Avery where to go. Abby was restless in her car seat, and when Lisa touched her cheek, it felt like it was on fire. Again, she called Andrew and left a message telling him which hospital they were going to.

"Isn't he answering?" Avery asked, sounding annoyed.

"No. He hasn't answered all evening. I've left a dozen messages." She saw Avery shaking his head but was thankful he didn't say what she suspected he was thinking. It didn't matter anyway. All that mattered was Abby.

Ten minutes later, Avery pulled the car up to the emergency room doors. "Go ahead in with Abby and I'll park the car. I'll catch up with you."

Lisa pulled Abby out of her car seat, wrapped the blanket around her, and ran inside.

Because of Abby's young age and the fact that her temperature registered at one-hundred and four, they took her in immediately. Lisa accompanied her into the exam room and watched, feeling helpless, as the nurses took Abby's vitals. As she waited for the doctor to come in, Avery came into the room.

"I hope you don't mind my being here. I asked where you'd gone, and they assumed I was Abby's father and let me come back here."

Exhausted and scared, Lisa wrapped her arms around Avery. "No. I don't mind at all. I'm glad you're here."

Avery hugged her back and for the first time since yesterday, Lisa calmed down. She'd been doing everything alone for so long that it felt good to have someone by her side.

The doctor came in and shook Lisa's hand. "I'm Dr. Jenson. Can you tell me what's been happening to our little patient?"

After Lisa explained how Abby had been feeling for the past two days, the doctor examined her. Abby had calmed down and just stared at the doctor with big, round eyes.

"She's dehydrated, and her fever is high," Dr. Jenson told Lisa. "I'd like to give her IV fluids and have her stay the night. We'll try to get her fever down by morning."

Lisa nodded her consent and the doctor left to give the orders. A nurse came in after that.

"We'll be transferring Abby up to the third floor. If you'd like to go there and wait, I'll take her up and get her settled."

Lisa hesitated, but having been a nurse in a clinic setting herself, she knew it was best to let them do their job. "Please get me as soon as she's in her room."

The nurse smiled. "We will. I promise."

Lisa kissed Abby on the cheek. "I'll see you in a few minutes, sweetie." Then she and Avery went out into the hall.

"You don't have to stay," Lisa told him as they walked to the elevator. "I'll be fine as long as I can be with Abby."

Avery draped his arm around her waist and drew her close.

"I'm not leaving you." He whispered the words in her ear and softly kissed her temple. All the anxiety of the night welled up, and she fell into him, grateful for his presence. "Thank you."

They rode up to the third floor and sat in a small waiting room near the nurse's station where Lisa was sure they would find her. Avery had placed his arm around the back of her chair, and she'd dropped her head on his shoulder. She was exhausted. And so, so worried. Abby had never been this sick before; had never spent a night away except at Andrew's. Lisa was afraid the little girl would be scared without her mommy nearby. She was anxious to get back to her daughter's side.

"She's going to be fine," Avery said softly, as if reading her thoughts.

"I know. It's just hard seeing Abby so sick."

"I know you did everything you could to take care of her. Sometimes we just can't do it ourselves. I'm sure she'll be up and chasing Bailey around in a day or two." He smiled over at her.

She nodded, unable to speak because of the lump forming in her throat. She was relieved that Avery had seen her leaving the house and had offered to drive her. She could have asked Kristen to come along, or Mallory, but she would rather be here with Avery and his calming presence. "Thank you for being here."

"I wouldn't want to be anywhere else," he said.

If she hadn't been so worried and tired, she would have found their situation amusing. Avery in his running pants and sweatshirt, her in a pair of yoga pants and an old T-shirt, sitting here in this sterile environment. She knew her hair was uncombed, and she didn't have a stitch of makeup on. Avery looked like he'd been running his hand through his hair as he wrote. They looked a mess, but who didn't at midnight?

"Were you writing when you saw us? Or watching us out your window again?"

Avery chuckled. "All of the above. I was worried about you and Abby. I couldn't sleep, so I tried writing. When I saw you come outside, I guessed what you were doing. I figured you weren't going for a midnight joyride."

"I'm glad you saw us. I don't know if I could have driven here, by myself. I was so upset."

"Hermits can be useful sometimes." He winked.

The nurse finally came and showed Lisa to Abby's room. The room was small, but private, with a single crib and a sofa that folded out as a bed. Abby was hooked up to an IV bottle, her little body looking pale under the fluorescent lights.

"She was a little trooper," the nurse said. "Hardly a peep out of her. Hopefully the fluids will help her feel better and then she'll be able to keep liquids down on her own. We've given her Motrin for the fever and will monitor that all night. For now, let's hope she gets some sleep."

"Thank you," Lisa said, relieved. She reached over the crib and took Abby's small hand. "You try to sleep, baby. Tomorrow will be better."

Abby was already having trouble keeping her eyes open. Soon, she fell to sleep, much to Lisa's relief.

Lisa sat down on the sofa and laid her head back. She was so tired. She couldn't remember ever feeling this drained.

Avery sat beside her and took her hand. "What can I do for you? Do you want something to eat or drink? Can I bring you anything from home?"

She turned to him, so grateful he was here. "I don't need anything but thank you. I think I'll try to sleep while Abby does. You should go home and get some sleep, too. But could you do me a favor?"

"Anything."

"Would you bring Bailey to your house for the night? He's going to go crazy with worry over Abby being away."

Avery smiled. "I can do that."

"Thank you. I don't know what I would have done without you here."

"You're more than welcome." Avery found a blanket in the closet and placed it over her. She felt herself drifting off, unable to stay awake any longer. He kissed her cheek. "See you in the morning," he whispered.

The last thing Lisa heard were his footsteps crossing the room before she fell into a deep sleep.

Chapter Thirteen

Avery was startled awake by something cold and wet touching his hand. He opened his eyes and there was Bailey, smiling up at him from the side of the bed.

"Hey, boy." Avery rubbed his hands over his face and looked at the clock. It was only seven in the morning. "You must be an early riser," he told the dog.

Moving slowly, Avery stood and slipped on his track pants from the night before. He couldn't believe how hard he'd slept after lying down last night. He'd come home and gone to Lisa's to get Bailey, then the two of them ate a midnight snack before heading to bed. Avery had thought he wouldn't be able to sleep because his mind was too wound up with worry for Abby. But he'd been so exhausted, he'd dropped off quickly.

"I'd better let you out," Avery told Bailey, "and make your breakfast." He let the dog into his backyard, which, luckily was fenced in, then walked to the kitchen to brew a cup of coffee. Last night he'd remembered to grab Bailey's bowls and a couple of cans of dog food, so he put some food in a bowl and set it down by the water, then let Bailey in.

"I'd better ask Lisa how much she normally feeds you; otherwise, I may be giving you too much."

Bailey looked at him like that wouldn't be a problem, which made Avery laugh.

After showering, Avery texted Lisa, asking how Abby was.

She's doing better. Fever is down and she has more energy. The doctor said she will release Abby today if she's still improving by noon. Lisa texted back.

"Your little girl is coming home," Avery told Bailey. "You're going to be a happy dog."

His phone rang then, and he answered it quickly because he saw it was Lisa.

"Hi."

"Hi. Can I ask another favor of you?" Lisa asked.

"Anything you want," he said, grinning to himself.

"Could you bring Abby's bag from the closet by the door? It's bright blue and has some clothes and other stuff in it. I don't want to bring her home in those sweaty pajamas."

"I can do that. What about you? Do you need a change of clothes?"

She laughed. "I'm not going to ask you to dig through my closet and pick out an outfit for me. But thanks for asking." He could imagine her smiling on the other end of the line.

"I'm ready to go. I'll just grab that bag and be there in a few minutes."

"Thanks. No rush, though. We're not leaving for a while."

They hung up and Avery ran across the street with Bailey following him. The morning was crisp, and the leaves had changed to even brighter reds and golds. It would be October in two days and soon the long, cold winter would come. Avery couldn't help but wonder what winter would hold for him this year. Last year he'd spent it alone in his house, writing and brooding. He hoped it wouldn't be the same this year, now that he'd finally come out of his cave.

He found Abby's bag in the closet and left Bailey at Lisa's house. As he walked outdoors again, Kristen flagged him down in the driveway.

"How's Abby? Is she feeling any better?"

"Lisa brought her to the hospital last night. She stayed overnight and they gave her fluids," Avery told her.

Kristen looked stunned. "I had no idea. Oh, that poor little girl. Is she better?"

"She's much better this morning. I just spoke to Lisa and she said they were talking of letting her come home today."

Kristen placed a hand on her chest, looking relieved. "I'm so glad to hear that." She glanced over and saw Lisa's car in his driveway. "Did you drive her to the hospital last night?"

"Yeah. I saw her come out to her car and rushed over. She wasn't in any condition to drive. She was so worried about Abby. I'm going there now to hopefully bring them home."

"I'm so glad you were there to help her. Please tell her I'm thinking about her and not to hesitate to ask for anything," Kristen said. She smiled. "You've turned out to be a really good guy."

He laughed. "I try."

Avery arrived at the hospital around nine and stopped by the gift shop and cafeteria before going up to Abby's room. When he walked in carrying the bag, two cups of coffee, some rolls, and a gift for Abby under his arm, Lisa smiled warmly.

"Do I smell coffee?"

"Yep." He set everything down and looked over the side of the crib. Abby was no longer hooked up to an IV and her color looked good. "Hey, sweetie. You're looking much better than last night."

Abby grinned. "Baywee?" she asked, hopeful.

"Bailey is waiting patiently at home for you," Avery said. "He sure has missed you." He handed Abby the little stuffed dog he'd found in the gift shop. It was black and white like Bailey, with blue eyes.

"Baywee!" she squealed, hugging the puppy.

"I thought you might need a stuffy to hug," he said.

"That was so sweet of you," Lisa said. "Thank you."

He winked. "I'll do anything for a smile."

They sat on the sofa and drank coffee and ate rolls. Lisa told Avery all about their night in the hospital. "Abby woke up a couple of times, but other than that, she actually slept well. Her temperature is back to normal, thank goodness."

"I'm glad to hear that. So, is she going home?"

"The doctor said yes. They'll be signing her out at noon."

"And what about you? Did you get any sleep last night?" Avery asked.

"I did. As much as possible. But I think Abby and I will both need a long nap when we get home." She grinned. "And a shower. I definitely need to clean up. I look like a disaster."

He reached up and pushed a strand of loose hair behind her ear. "You look beautiful," he said tenderly. He watched as her face blushed pink. He'd meant what he'd said. She looked just as beautiful to him today as she had the other night when they'd gone on their date. He liked the spray of freckles that dusted her nose and cheeks and how her lashes framed her blue eyes. She didn't need a lot of makeup to be lovely. Her sweetness shone through from the inside out.

"You need glasses," she teased.

He chuckled, then turned serious. "I told Kristen you were here with Abby. She was happy to hear that Abby was doing better."

"I should have called her, but time just slipped by. And Andrew never called me back. It's so frustrating that he isn't available when Abby needs him."

"Maybe he'll call today," Avery offered, although he doubted the guy would. He seemed like a selfish jerk, but he kept that thought to himself.

Lisa shrugged. "I tried to keep him informed. I don't owe him anything more than that."

They sat there a while longer before the doctor came and checked on Abby. Then the nurse brought in instructions and the release papers. "If her fever spikes again, bring her back. Or if she becomes dehydrated again. But it looks like she's on the mend, so hopefully we won't see her in here again."

Lisa thanked her then took out some fresh clothes from the bag Avery had brought and changed Abby.

"Ready to go home?" Avery asked.

"Most definitely yes," Lisa told him.

* * *

Lisa was happy to be home. Abby had perked up a little and even squealed with delight and hugged Bailey when she saw him.

Avery hovered near the door. "Well, I guess it's time I get back to writing. Let me know if I can do anything for you."

Lisa walked over close to him. "You've done so much already. Thank you for being there when we needed you most."

"I was happy to help." He moved even closer to her and slipped his arms around her waist. "We never had a chance to finish our date. Maybe we can do that sometime soon, when Abby is better."

She gazed at him, her face only inches from his. He'd shaved this morning and it made him look younger than when he'd been a scruffy hermit. She liked how kind his face looked. "I'd like that."

Avery bent his head as if he were going to kiss her, but she pulled back and laughed. "I haven't brushed my teeth in two days."

"I don't care," he murmured. Frankly, neither did she. Just as their lips touched, there was a knock coming from the kitchen door. Avery groaned.

"I'll bet that's Kristen checking up on Abby," Lisa said.

He pulled away but was smiling. "I'll take a raincheck on that kiss. Someday, it's going to happen."

The anticipation of that kiss gave Lisa delightful goosebumps.

She waved as he left then headed to the kitchen. Kristen was on the stoop, carrying a basket and a jar of soup.

"I was so worried," Kristen said as she came inside. "I'm glad you're home. I brought you some muffins and soup, so you don't have to worry about making dinner tonight."

Lisa's heart swelled. She loved how kind and caring her neighbors were. She adored her sweet little neighborhood. And she was beginning to fall for a certain handsome hermit from across the street.

Monday morning, Lisa called in to work to take a personal day and kept Abby home, just to make sure she was feeling okay. The fever hadn't returned the night before, and the little girl was already eating well and regaining her energy. Lisa couldn't believe how easily she'd bounced back from her illness. She wished she had half of Abby's energy.

Andrew finally called around eleven o'clock. "How is Abby? Are you home or still at the hospital?" To his credit, he sounded worried, but as far as Lisa was concerned, it was too little, too late.

"She's home and feeling better. I kept her home today," she told him.

Andrew sighed heavily. "So, was this a false alarm? Were all those messages you left me for nothing?"

Anger swelled up inside Lisa. "No, it wasn't a false alarm. I called because I thought you'd want to know your daughter was in the hospital with a fever of a hundred and four and getting IV fluids."

"But she's better now, right? She's no longer sick."

"She's getting better," Lisa said. "But that doesn't mean she wasn't sick. Why didn't you answer your phone all weekend? This was an emergency and you should have been there for her."

"I had my phone turned off. It wasn't my idea, believe me. Kat wanted time away from everything and I agreed. We went up to the North Shore for a couple of days."

Lisa's anger grew. "Well, as long as it was important," she said snidely. "I wouldn't have wanted to ruin your weekend trip with something as trivial as your daughter being in the hospital."

"That's not fair and you know it," he said angrily. "I won't be made to feel guilty when it's not my weekend to have Abby. She was your responsibility."

"She's always my responsibility!" Her voice rose. "And if you want to have shared custody, you should be available to her all the time too."

There was a long pause as Lisa waited for Andrew to make more excuses. To her surprise, he conceded.

"You're right," he said, his voice calmer. "I shouldn't have turned off my phone. It won't happen again. It's just that things have been a little tense between Kat and me and she wanted my full attention. But she'll have to accept the fact that Abby comes first. I'm sorry."

Lisa thought she was going to fall over when she heard him apologize. Andrew never took the blame for anything. It had been one of the many things about him that had driven her crazy while they were married.

"Okay," she said, also calming down. "I'll admit I went overboard with the messages, but I was so scared. Abby has never been that sick before. Even though I'm a nurse, it's different when it's your own child."

"I'm sorry you had to do this alone. That's not fair, and I get it. I should have been there for you."

"I wasn't alone. In fact, I was lucky that Avery saw me putting Abby in the car and he rushed over and drove me there. I was in no frame of mind to drive, especially in the middle of the night. He stayed with me, too, until the hospital settled Abby in a room."

Lisa didn't know why she'd told Andrew about Avery driving her. Some part of her wanted to let him know that she also had someone who cared about her. Maybe she wanted to rub it in a little, even though she knew she shouldn't.

"Avery?" Andrew asked, sounding confused. "Who's that?"

"You've met him. He fixed the back fence so Bailey wouldn't dig under it."

"The gardener?" he asked with disdain.

"He's not a gardener. He's a writer. And he's been very helpful this past couple of weeks. You should be thanking him instead of being so snide."

"What in the world was this guy doing up at midnight, watching your house? He sounds like a creep."

Once again, Andrew made her blood boil. "He's not a creep. He's a nice guy. At least he was there for me and Abby, and you weren't."

After another minute or two of sparring, Andrew said goodbye. But not before reminding Lisa that he had Abby this upcoming weekend. Lisa sighed when she hit the off button. She watched her daughter as the little girl played with a pile of toys and dolls on the floor with Bailey lying beside her. Every so often, Abby would pat the dog on the back before returning to playing. This made Lisa smile. Some children had a favorite stuffed toy, others had a blanket, but Abby had Bailey. He was her security blanket, her favorite lovey. The thought of Abby being so sick made her stomach churn. What would she have done if she lost Abby? Lisa didn't know if she could recover from that, ever.

She went over and sat down beside Abby on the floor and the two began playing with a simple puzzle. Moments like this were few and far between now that Lisa worked full-time. She had to enjoy every moment she could before the years piled up unexpectedly and Abby was grown and gone. Then what? Lisa had thought she'd spend her life with Andrew: they'd grow old together, retire, and travel. That dream was gone. Maybe it was time to think of a new dream.

Unexpectedly, Avery's face came to mind. She smiled. She thought back to yesterday morning when he'd tucked a strand of hair behind her ear and told her she looked beautiful. Her heart had melted as a blush had crept up her face. He couldn't have said anything sweeter at that moment, after the long night she'd had. He truly was a romantic, and that was something she needed in her life right now. Someone who cared enough about her to see her amongst all the chaos going on around her.

And despite the rocky start between the two of them, he did see her.

She ran her hand through her daughter's silky hair. "We really are very lucky. You know that, sweetie?"

Abby smiled that precious toddler smile up at her and Bailey did the same. Lisa's life was full.

Chapter Fourteen

The week sped by for Lisa. Avery came over a couple of nights for dinner, one night with pizza for them and spaghetti for Abby. Otherwise, Lisa hadn't seen much of him because their lives were so busy. He said he'd been writing non-stop since bringing them home from the hospital and didn't want to break his rhythm. Lisa had no understanding of the creative process of writing a book, and she was impressed by his self-motivation to be able to sit down for hours, typing. She knew she'd be distracted by a hundred different things; although she had a child and dog while Avery was home alone. That made a big difference.

Lisa had also made a difficult decision to call her lawyer and explain how Andrew hadn't made himself available when there'd been a health emergency for Abby. She knew she was being catty, yet also knew that Andrew would use whatever ammunition he could find against her. The lawyer said he'd speak with the judge about this new development before the ruling next Wednesday. He thought it might make a difference in their case.

Thursday night, Andrew texted her that he'd be picking Abby up, as usual, on Friday at five-thirty. She wanted to tell him no but knew she couldn't. Abby was feeling better and he had a right to see her on his designated weekends. But after

Abby had been sick last week, Lisa felt extra protective of her. She wanted to keep her safe from everything, even though that wasn't possible. Kids got sick all the time, and she knew that better than anyone because of the job she held. But it was still hard not to worry.

Andrew arrived on time Friday evening, as always. Lisa opened the door and saw Avery coming into the yard with Bailey, returning the dog after a walk, as Andrew stepped out of his car.

"Now you're the dog walker?" Andrew said snidely to Avery.

Avery only stared at him with his brow puckered, then turned and headed for the backyard without responding. Lisa was so proud of him for being the bigger man.

"Andrew! What's wrong with you? You're acting like you're in second grade," Lisa said as he stepped onto the porch.

Andrew wrinkled his nose. "Is Abby ready?"

"Yes. Isn't she always? We rush around trying to be ready when you come." Lisa had said the words more harshly than she'd meant, but Andrew had angered her with the comment he'd made to Avery.

"Then let's go. Abby!" he called over Lisa's shoulder. "Let's get going, sweetheart."

Lisa ran to get Abby's small suitcase and toy bag as Andrew came inside to lift Abby into his arms. When Lisa returned, she handed the bags to Andrew and gave Abby a kiss on the cheek.

"You be a good girl for Daddy," she said. "I'll see you very soon." To her relief, Abby didn't seem too upset that Andrew was taking her away. She walked them to the door, and that was when she noticed that Katrina wasn't in the car, waiting.

"Where's Katrina?"

Andrew's face creased into a frown. "She's away for the weekend. It'll just be me and Abby this time." He continued to the car and Lisa followed. She wasn't a big fan of Katrina, but she'd always thought it was better for Abby if both of them were there, watching her. "Will you be okay with Abby by yourself?"

He stopped buckling Abby into the car seat, turned, and glared at Lisa. "Of course we'll be okay. She's my daughter. It's not like Kat did anything to help anyway."

"Sheesh. Fine. I just figured she helped you a little, that's all."

Andrew took a deep breath and let out a sigh. "Sorry. I didn't mean to yell. We'll be fine. In fact, it'll be better without Kat's whining for a change." He finished buckling Abby in and was about to close the door when the little girl reached out her hands and said, "Baywee?"

"No, dear. The dog can't come," Andrew told her.

Lisa thought a moment, then told Andrew to wait a moment. She ran into the house and came out with the stuffed dog that looked like Bailey. "Here, sweetie."

Abby took the dog and hugged it tight.

"I figured that was what she meant," Lisa said.

"Where'd she get that?" Andrew asked.

"Avery bought it for her while she was in the hospital. She adores it."

"Cripes. Is that guy always around?" Andrew asked, looking disgusted.

"Is it any of your business?"

Andrew lifted his hand, palm up, as if to ward off her words. "Fine. I don't care. Date the gardener or dog walker or whatever he is." He stalked around to the other side of the car to get in.

Lisa smiled down at Abby. "Have a good time, sweetie." She shut the door and waved as Andrew pulled away.

When she got back to the house, Avery was standing on the front porch with his arms crossed.

"Is he always such a nightmare?"

She laughed. "He wasn't when I first met him. But now, yeah."

He smiled and wrapped his arms around her waist, bringing her close. "So. You're all alone for the whole weekend."

"Looks that way. Well, except for Bailey."

"You've had a long week. Would you like to go out for dinner? Maybe to Gallagher's?"

She reached her arms up and wrapped them around his neck. He was the perfect height for her. They fit well together. "I would love to go to Gallagher's. And then what?"

He waggled his brows, which made her laugh. "I'm sure, as an expert romance writer, I could think of something." He slowly lowered his head and their lips were just about to meet when she pulled away and grinned.

"You have to feed me first, Mr. Romance. I'm starving."

Avery laughed. "Okay. Fine. But the next time I get you in my arms, I'm not letting you go."

"Is that a promise?"

His eyes sparkled. "Tease."

She chuckled and headed inside to change.

* * *

An hour later, Andrew and Lisa were sitting in a corner booth at Gallagher's and both had ordered a beer on tap while they waited for their food. James came over for a few minutes to chat, then returned to bartending.

Avery smiled over at Lisa. She looked pretty with her long hair down, and her eyes reflected the blue of her sweater. He knew she'd had a rough week, but she looked more rested today. Although to him, she was beautiful no matter what.

"Alone at last," Avery said, waggling his brows suggestively.

"Well, sort of." She glanced around the busy pub to make her point.

"I'll take whatever I can get," he said. "Not to ruin the moment, but what was up with Andrew?"

She sighed. "He and Katrina are having problems, I guess. They'd gone away for the weekend last week, so that was why I couldn't get ahold of him. Now, he said she was gone this weekend. He had a little fit when I suggested it might be harder to have Abby without Katrina's help."

"Hm. Trouble in paradise, huh? Well, that will teach him."

"Teach him what?"

Avery reached across the table and took her hand in his. "Not to toss away a diamond for a zirconia."

She smiled, and he detected a flush on her cheeks. "How do you know I'm not a zirconia, too?"

He leaned in closer to her. "Because I've seen you shine and sparkle and how tough yet beautiful you can be. I know you're the real thing, not a cheap imitation."

"You're sweet."

"I am, aren't I?" He winked.

Their food came and they spent the next hour talking about work, his book, and how Bailey was doing on his walks. At the mention of walking, Avery asked, "Would you like to go walking tomorrow if the weather isn't too cold?"

"Sure. Do you want to go to Lake Harriet again, or take the trail to Lake Calhoun?"

His eyes twinkled with mischief. "I thought we'd go to Lake Harriet. In fact, I made an appointment to see a house there. My house. Do you want to take a tour?"

"Your house? Really? Are we breaking in or did you call a realtor?"

"Is it breaking in if I have a key?" He grinned at her shocked expression. "I'm just kidding. I'm meeting a realtor. I want to see what Melissa left inside. And I may be in the market to buy it if this book pans out."

Lisa cocked her head and looked at him curiously. "Didn't the realtor know it was your house? And wouldn't that bring up a red flag?"

He shook his head. "She didn't know. Melissa is using her maiden name now, so the realtor didn't know Avery McKinnon had owned the house. She recognized my name as an author and was thrilled I wanted to look at it. I guess the house hasn't had too many bites."

"Those houses are expensive. I'm sure it has to be the right person to buy it," Lisa said.

"I think I'm the right person. I loved that house. But I'm actually loving the neighborhood I'm in now, so it might be a tough decision."

"Is there a reason you've suddenly fallen in love with your neighborhood?" Lisa asked, looking coy.

"Yes. Everyone loves dogs there. How can I not like a neighborhood that loves dogs?"

Lisa rolled her eyes. "Well, that's true. I don't trust people who hate dogs."

He leaned on the table and whispered. "Plus, there's this really pretty blonde there. But don't tell her I think she's cute. She'll probably get a big head."

Lisa chuckled. "I doubt that."

As they were finishing their meal, Avery looked up as a shadow fell across him. To his horror, Melissa was standing there with Ross Gunderson behind her.

"Imagine seeing you in here again so soon," Melissa said, her glossy red lips curving into an evil Disney queen smile.

Avery glowered at her. "What do you want? Oh, yeah. You have everything I own, so there's nothing else I can give."

"Very funny." She turned to Lisa, extending her hand. "Hi. I'm Melissa, his ex. Who are you?"

Lisa shook it. "I'm Lisa. I live across the street from Avery."

"Lucky you," Melissa said sarcastically. She gave Lisa the once-over then dismissed her by turning toward Avery again. "So. Have you thought about my offer?"

"Offer?" Avery snorted. "You mean the chance for you to extort more money from me? No thanks."

Melissa's eyes narrowed as her face took on a truly scary look. "Fine. I guess you'll never see your dog again. Have a nice night." She grabbed Ross's hand and pulled him toward the door.

Avery felt his blood burning in his veins. He stood and yelled, "Go to hell, Cruella!"

Melissa stopped at the entrance and turned, tossing him a deadly glare. Then she and her boyfriend were gone.

James rushed over to the table. "Cripes, Avery. What was that all about? I thought I'd have to come up here and break up a brawl between you and that woman."

Avery took a deep breath and let it out. Slowly, his anger abated. "Sorry, James. That was my ex-wife. She was trying to make me angry, and it worked."

James slapped him on the back. "We all have someone like that in our past. You can calm down now. She's gone." He gave them one of his infectious grins then left.

Avery sat down. "Sorry. I shouldn't have taken her bait."

"It's okay. I get it. Andrew does that to me, too."

Avery drank down the last of his beer and put money in the folder for the food. "Ready to go?"

"Yes." She chuckled.

"What?"

"Cruella?"

Avery grinned. "Well, she is. She's holding my dog hostage against her will." He slipped his arm around her waist and they headed to the door, waving to James. When they got to the car, Avery turned to Lisa. "Now. About that kiss."

She grinned. "Take me home, Mr. Romance."

"Okay. But you don't know what you're missing out on."

She looked at him tenderly. "Believe me, I do." They got in the car and headed home.

* * *

The next morning, Avery awoke with a smile on his lips. He was going to spend the day with Lisa. Last night, she had been yawning on the way home, and he knew she was beat, so he'd said goodnight at her door to let her get some sleep. And even though he had yet to kiss her, it didn't matter. Because she was worth the wait. He'd lived a year in a sour mood, and she'd been the one to break it. He could wait a little longer for that first kiss.

But hopefully not too long.

He'd worked late into the night on his manuscript and it was slowly turning into a story he loved. Hopefully, his agent and publisher would love it too. It wasn't the story he'd outlined and sold to them, but it was a better story, an unforgettable story like the ones he wrote at the beginning of his career. He was writing from the heart, like he'd done before when he'd been insanely in love. This time though, Melissa wasn't his muse. Lisa was.

Which meant he was falling hard for her. A scary yet thrilling thought.

He let that wash over him as he showered and dressed. The more he thought of it, the better it felt. But, he wondered, did *she* like *him* that way?

He wouldn't even entertain that thought. Lisa had been teasing him and gently flirting, so there must be a spark for her too. They had time to figure it all out. Something this good was worth taking slowly.

He arrived on Lisa's doorstep at noon. They were meeting the realtor at one, so that gave them an hour to take a leisurely walk.

"Hey there," she said, letting him inside. Bailey came running and Avery placed his hand down to stop the dog from jumping. Bailey stopped and sat, but his tail wagged vigorously with happiness. Avery laughed and bent down to pet him. "Hey there to you, too."

"Ready to go walking?" Lisa asked. She had Bailey's harness on and was already holding his leash.

"Yes. If you're ready, let's go."

"Should I bring water?" she asked.

He motioned to the backpack he was wearing. "I have all we need." He took the leash and clipped it on Bailey. "Okay, boy. Show Lisa what you've learned. Make me look good, okay?" He winked at Lisa, which made her smile.

They took their time walking through their own neighborhood, enjoying the colorful leaves on the trees. They turned down one street, then another, until they were across from Lake Harriet. Avery's former house was a few blocks away, so they meandered down the street. Many of the homes had mature trees and large bushes that gave privacy. The leaves had turned golden hues as well as fiery reds and brilliant oranges. It was a beautiful time of year to admire these mansions that had graced the street since the 1920s.

"My house was built in 1922," Avery told her as they walked toward it. "Those were the days when they put a fireplace in every room and added beautiful details, much like your Craftsman-style home, except a lot bigger."

"I can imagine," Lisa said.

"Even though a previous owner had updated the home, it still has some of that old charm. All the light fixtures are original. They were converted from gas to electric. And there's woodwork in the study that's gorgeous. The floors are original, too, except they'd been stained a darker color by the time I purchased it."

"How long did you live there?" Lisa asked.

"Only four years, but I just loved it so much. After my first two novels took off, my publisher offered me a four book, seven-figure contract. My agent said they were afraid I'd leave for a bigger publishing house. That's when I bought the house. I'd still be in there, too, if Melissa hadn't taken it."

Lisa was looking at him with wide eyes. "Seven-figures? I guessed you made good money, but I hadn't realized it was that much."

Avery was immediately sorry he'd told her. Lisa wasn't one to be dazzled by money, and he hoped he hadn't sounded like he was bragging. "I was lucky, I guess," he said quickly. "Not every author gets a deal like that. And I'm not sure I'll ever get a deal like that again. But I'm hoping this latest novel will do the trick."

"I can't even imagine that much money," she said. "But good for you. Your books are worth it."

"Thanks." It pleased him that she felt that way.

They finally came to his former house and stood on the sidewalk a moment to admire it. The house sat on a hill, with brick stairs that led up to the yard. Trees and shrubs hid most of the house from view.

"It's a Tudor style, like Mallory and James's house," Lisa said, smiling. "Well, except ten times bigger, I'd guess."

"It's about six-thousand square feet," Avery said. "So, yeah. There's a lot of room."

"Wow. What do you do with all that space?"

Avery shrugged. "You find uses for it. I miss having a real office space, and my gym. And the pool. I really miss the pool."

"There's a pool, too?" Lisa looked stunned.

"Ah, yeah." Avery was realizing just how spoiled he sounded.

A car pulled up behind them and they turned to look. A woman in a tan suit with auburn hair stepped out and smiled at them. "Are you Avery McKinnon?"

"Yes." Avery lifted his hand to shake hers.

"Candace Greenfield," she said. "It's nice to meet you. I've read all your books but have never seen a picture of you on any of them. I'm afraid to admit that I thought you were a woman."

Lisa chuckled. "I did too."

"This is Lisa Evans," Avery said.

The women shook hands, then Candace looked down at Bailey. "And who's this?"

"This is Bailey," Avery said. "We decided to walk here and brought him along. I hope you don't mind."

"Of course not. He seems like a well-behaved dog," the realtor said.

Lisa grimaced at Avery and he nearly laughed out loud. "Yes. He is. Shall we go inside?"

Candace led the way and opened the heavy wooden door for them. They walked into a beautifully tiled entryway then through a mahogany framed door with etched glass that led to the main hall. A staircase with mahogany steps and railings rose from the center. The formal living room was on the right and the dining room was to the left. The ceiling here was extremely tall, and Avery watched as Lisa craned her neck to look at the chandelier that hung from the center.

"This is beautiful," Lisa said, sounding impressed.

"And we're only in the entryway." Avery chuckled.

"Why don't you look around the lower floor and I'll meet you here by the stairs," Candace suggested.

"Sounds good." Avery led Lisa through the dining room first, then on to the kitchen. He unhooked Bailey's leash and let him out the back door into the yard.

"He can't run away, can he?" Lisa looked concerned.

"Nope. It's fenced in. You just can't tell there's a fence because it's hidden behind shrubs and trees."

Lisa looked at Avery curiously. "The living and dining room furniture doesn't really look like your style."

Avery cocked his head. "And what style is that?"

"I don't know. You dress so casual with flannel shirts and T-shirts and you wear cowboy boots when you do dress up. I figured you would be more of a lodge or country style. This furniture looks like something a decorator would choose."

"Well, you're right about that. Melissa chose most of the furnishings with the help of a decorator. Like the living room. It's all white. I would have done natural tones. But the kitchen is beautiful, don't you think?"

The kitchen cabinets were an antique white with dark quartz countertops and a mahogany wood floor. It was large—a lot of counterspace and cabinets with a huge island that also had a sink and second oven. To the side of it was a good-sized family room with a stone fireplace, a big bay window, and leather sofas and chairs.

"I love the kitchen," Lisa said. "And the family room is more casual, which I like. But jeez. I could fit my whole house in these two rooms."

Avery laughed. "Not quite. But it's roomy."

They went through the home gym at the back of the house and then into the office which had dark woodwork, built-in shelves, and large windows. Lisa admired the view of the park and lake. "I'll bet you enjoyed this view while you worked better than the view you have now."

Avery grinned. "It is a beautiful view, but so is the one I have now." He winked and saw Lisa's cheeks grow pink.

From there they circled around into the formal living room that, as Avery had mentioned, was done all in white.

"Any questions yet?" the realtor asked as they came back to the stairs.

"Not yet. Can we go upstairs?" Avery asked.

"Of course. Go ahead and I'll wait down here."

They toured the upstairs where Lisa continued to look around in wide-eyed wonder. Avery felt proud of the fact that he'd owned this beautiful house, and he really wanted Lisa to like it. When they stopped for a moment in the master bedroom, that had a brick fireplace and a four-poster bed as well as a huge master bath, Avery led her to the bay window.

"Now, that's a view. Don't you think?" he asked. Out the window was a gorgeous panorama of Lake Harriet, the surrounding trees in shades of red, orange, and yellow.

"It's beautiful," Lisa told him. "Absolutely amazing."

He took her down the back staircase that led to the kitchen and showed her the pool in the backyard. It hadn't been drained yet for winter, and the water sparkled in the afternoon sunshine.

"Wouldn't Abby love swimming in that all summer?" he asked.

"She definitely would," Lisa said without enthusiasm.

Avery was disappointed that Lisa didn't sound very excited.

Bailey came running to them and Avery snapped his leash on. They went back to the front where Candace was waiting.

"Thank you for showing us the house," Avery said, shaking her hand again. "Do you think there's any chance the owner would sell for a little less?"

"It never hurts to place a bid and try." Candace handed him her card. "Let me know if you'd like to look at other houses around here or bid on this one."

"I will," he said. They left and began walking toward the lake.

"Do you think you might buy it back?" Lisa asked as they walked.

Avery shrugged. "I'm not sure. If Melissa knew it was me, she'd be a bear to deal with. Besides, I'll have to wait and see if my publisher signs me again after this book is turned in. I doubt the house will sell anytime soon."

Lisa nodded. She slowed to a stop and looked at him. "Do you mind if we just walk home? I have a lot to do today and I'm a little tired."

"Oh. Okay. Sure." They turned back in the direction of their houses. Lisa was quiet for much of the walk and Avery didn't press her. He wasn't sure if she was overwhelmed by seeing the house or thought that maybe he was bragging. He hadn't meant to sound that way; he'd only wanted her to see where he'd once lived. As they came to her house, she took Bailey's leash.

"Would you like to grab a burger later? Or maybe we could order in pizza," he said. He had hoped to spend the evening with her.

"Ah, okay. Maybe. Why don't you text me later then we can decide," she told him.

"Lisa? Is something wrong?" He wasn't sure what he'd done for her to turn cold on him.

"No. I just have some things to do. I'll talk to you later." She waved and entered the house with Bailey following behind her.

Chapter Fifteen

Lisa worked around the house all afternoon doing laundry, changing sheets, and cleaning out the fridge. But the entire time, all she thought about was that amazing house and the fact that Avery earned seven figures. Seven figures! She couldn't even imagine earning that kind of money. She'd known he was a successful author, but hadn't really thought about the amount of money he earned. Seven figures was way out of her league.

When she'd first seen Avery move into the bungalow a year ago, she'd thought he was the same as everyone else in this neighborhood. A hard-working, middle-income kind of guy. This wasn't a fancy neighborhood, but it was a nice one where people were friendly and everyone took pride in their homes. But now she knew he was used to the finer things in life, and for some reason, that bothered her. It made her look closely at herself, and she found herself lacking. She wasn't beautiful, she had never been rich, and she wouldn't have the faintest idea what to do with a house that large. So why was a guy like Avery interested in her?

Kristen knocked on her kitchen door later that afternoon, bringing a jar of her homemade chicken dumpling soup. "I suppose this is Andrew's weekend with Abby," she said as Lisa let her into the kitchen.

"Yes. I was a little scared of letting her go after having been so sick, but I had no choice."

"I saw you and Avery walking earlier today. Did you have a good time?"

Lisa invited Kristen to sit at the small kitchen table and offered her a soda, which she accepted. "Yes and no."

Kristen's eyebrows rose.

"We went on a tour of his former house. It's for sale. His wife got it in the divorce and is now selling it."

"Oh. That's terrible. Does he want to buy it back?"

"Maybe. He's thinking about it. It's one of the mansions across the street from Lake Harriet," Lisa said.

"Wow. That's neat. What did it look like?"

Lisa shrugged. "Like a beautiful mansion. It had tons of room, antique woodwork and light fixtures, a huge kitchen, and a pool."

"Goodness." Kristen looked impressed. "I never thought he made that kind of money, but I suppose he does. It just never occurred to me."

"Me neither. He was just the hermit across the street, living in the cute bungalow house."

Kristen looked at her curiously. "I take it you weren't impressed."

"I was," Lisa said. "But it was overwhelming, too. I mean, it wasn't like he was trying to impress me; he was so used to living that way he was just showing me the house. Like it was natural for him. But for me, it seemed over-the-top."

Kristen smiled. "So, you're thinking: Why does a guy like him want an everyday woman like me?"

Lisa's eyes grew wide. "Yes. How did you know? Is it so obvious I don't belong in a place like that?"

Kristen shook her head and placed her hand on Lisa's arm. "No. It's not obvious. I can see it in your eyes, though. I was in the same position once. When I first moved into this house, I was dating a very successful surgeon who was older than I was. He and I dated for a couple of years. He lived the high life and I never really fit in. But he wore his money on his sleeve, unlike Avery. He seems to act more like an everyday guy."

"So what's the moral of the story?" Lisa asked.

"There is no moral. I picked Ryan because we both had the same ideals about life, and plus he's adorable." She laughed. "You have to choose someone based on who they are, not what they have. If you're comfortable with Avery, and you like who he is, does it matter what he owns or where he lives?"

"You're right. It shouldn't matter. And I do like Avery. He seems like a good guy. I guess I just let everything overwhelm me. I do that sometimes."

Kristen stood and hugged Lisa. "You're doing a pretty amazing job of everything from what I've seen. You've only been divorced a few months, and you've been a working mom for a little over a month. You're doing great."

"Thanks. Sometimes, I feel like I'm drowning."

"Call any time you need a life preserver. I'll be here. And speaking of life savers, I'd better get back home and save Ryan. Marie had him playing princess as I was heading out the door."

Lisa laughed at the thought of Ryan in a princess dress. "You picked a winner there, that's for sure."

"I like to think so." She waved and left.

Lisa thought about what Kristen had said, and she agreed with her. She'd put too much emphasis on what Avery owned and not on who he was. So, when he texted an hour later, asking if she'd like to grab a burger at the local pub for dinner, she said yes.

* * *

Avery picked her up at six and they drove the couple of blocks to the pub where they'd eaten together the first time. Lisa sat silently in the car, not sure what to say to break the ice. So, neither of them said a word. Once they were at a table and had ordered their drinks, Avery finally spoke.

"I'm sorry if I made you uncomfortable today or if I came off as bragging by showing you the house. I was just excited for you to see it, but once I thought about it, I realized you may have thought I was being a jerk."

Lisa was shocked. She felt bad because she'd made him feel that way. "Don't apologize. I didn't think you were bragging at all. I was the one with the problem, not you."

He looked confused. "Why?"

Lisa sighed. "You were right about me feeling uncomfortable, but it wasn't your fault. The whole time we were looking at the house, and you were so excited about it, I was just trying to wrap my head around the fact that you had owned that house. I've only seen you as the guy in the bungalow across the street. An everyday guy, not a rich one. I had trouble picturing you living such an extravagant life, but you seemed so comfortable about it. It brought out all kinds of insecurities in me."

"You? Insecure? You're the strongest person I know."

She gave him a small smile. "No, I'm not. Kristen is strong. And so is Mallory. I know at least a dozen women who are so much stronger than me. I'm trying to be strong, but I feel like I'm failing every step of the way."

The waitress approached their table with their drinks and took their food order. After she left, Avery leaned in closer across the table. "You're not failing. You're doing a great job with Abby and you're handling going to work every day like a pro. You're also being strong dealing with Andrew."

Lisa shook her head. "I needed you to fix my yard so Bailey wouldn't run away. I needed Ryan to save me from the evil hermit across the street, and I needed Kristen today to show me that my issues with your wealth were unfounded. I can't seem to do anything on my own, no matter how hard I try."

Avery laughed. "I'm glad Ryan came over that day and told me off. If he hadn't, I wouldn't have gotten to know you better, nor would I have stepped out of my protective shell. You did that. You, and Bailey."

She smiled. She wasn't sure if that was true, but it was a nice thought. "Anyway, I'm sorry I acted so weird today. And I do think your house is beautiful. You'd be lucky to have it again. Anyone would be lucky to live in such a nice house."

Avery studied her a moment as he took a sip of his beer. "You know, we kind of started this whole friendship in the middle instead of at the beginning. We don't know that much about each other. Tell me about little Lisa and how you came to be who you are. Did you grow up here in Minneapolis?"

Lisa thought it was a good idea to share their stories. She knew so little about who Avery was and where he'd come from too. "I grew up in La Crosse, Wisconsin actually. My dad was a high school science teacher and my mom worked in a home for the disabled. My sister is five years older than me, so we were never very close. She's married and lives in California now."

"You said your dad *was* a teacher. Is he retired now?"

She nodded. "My mother died of cancer when I was fifteen. She'd been sick for a few years. When I graduated, I wanted to go to school away from home, so I went to the University of Minnesota. While I was in college, my father met another woman. Janice. She's nice, and I get along well with her. He retired after thirty years and moved to Sedona, Arizona. I only see them about once a year."

"I'm sorry about your mother," he said. "Is that why you became a nurse?"

"I'm not sure. Everyone thinks that, even my father, but I never related becoming a nurse to helping care for my mother. My mom was so strong, and she tried to stay independent of help for as long as she could. I always admired her strength. It couldn't have been easy. My sister is strong like that. I've never been like them. I feel like I've always had to lean on someone, and it's not my favorite trait."

Their burgers and fries came then, and they took a few bites. "This is good," Lisa said. "I didn't realize how hungry I was."

"Me, too. It's been a long day." He smiled at her. "You know, I don't think of you as someone who needs to lean on people. You let people help you, but that's okay. That's not the same as always needing someone to lean on."

"Maybe." She turned the focus back on him. "What about you? Are you from Minnesota?"

"Yep. Born and bred." He laughed. "I grew up in St. Cloud, had a normal childhood playing baseball and basketball until high school. My parents both worked. My father owned his own construction company, and my mom was an accountant in a local CPA firm. They spoiled me rotten and encouraged me to do whatever I wanted. When I said I wanted to go to college for journalism, they thought it was a good idea."

"Wow. The perfect childhood. Did you have any siblings?"

He shook his head. "No. I'm an only child. My parents were older when they had me. They had given up on ever having

children when I came as a surprise. That's why they spoiled me."
He grinned.

"You don't seem *that* spoiled," she said. She took another bite
of her burger, then asked, "What college did you attend?"

"I went to UMD."

"Really? Why Duluth and not Minneapolis?"

"I liked it there. It has the feel of a small town, yet it's big,
too. Plus, like you, I wanted to go to school away from home."

"Ah. I get it. What about your parents? Are they still in St.
Cloud?"

"No. They headed for a warmer climate. They live in Panama
City, Florida. I try to get down there a couple of times a year.
They're both in their late seventies now, so they don't come back
here anymore. Not that they're old—they walk the beach all the
time and keep busy. I can't keep up with them when I visit." He
chuckled.

"They sound great," she said, smiling.

"Well, maybe you'll get to meet them someday," he said,
winking.

After they finished eating, they sat for a while as the conversation flowed. Avery asked her about Andrew. "How did you two
meet?"

"At a college party," she said.

"I'll bet he was a frat boy." Avery grimaced.

"No." She laughed. "But he did the party circuit. I went with
a couple of girlfriends to a party at someone's house and he was
there. He was actually a gentleman. When my friends didn't
want to leave, he offered to walk me to my place. He was a junior
and I was a sophomore. We didn't actually start dating seriously
until his last year of college."

"So, before you finished college, you knew already that you

were going to marry him?"

"I guess so," she said. She'd never really thought of it that way before. "We started living together in my last year of college. He was working, and after I graduated, I was hired on at the hospital. We just kind of stayed together and then one day he proposed. It was a surprise, but I guess I'd figured we'd marry eventually. We just seemed to work well together."

"It's weird how relationships fall apart. You think you're together for the long haul, then one day, it's over."

Lisa thought back to the day she realized her marriage had fallen apart. It had seemed like it happened all at once, but when she thought back, it was a slow progression. She never really knew why Andrew had started looking at other women, or why he'd hooked up with Katrina. When he'd left, she'd been blindsided.

"What about you?" she asked, not wanting to talk about herself any longer. "How did you meet Melissa?"

"Ah. Melissa. I was working for a newspaper and also free-lancing, selling articles to magazines and websites. I wasn't doing too bad, income-wise, but my dream was to write a novel. I'd just written my first novel that no agent wanted when I met Melissa. She was a hostess in a fancy restaurant downtown. The type of restaurant where you have to call for reservations months in advance. An agent invited me to dinner to talk about my work, and that's when I met her. That long, silky hair and those gorgeous legs threw me for a loop. I admit it, her looks attracted me first, her personality second."

Lisa snorted. "Isn't that the way it is for most men?"

"Probably. Anyway, the agent didn't pan out, but he gave me some advice. He suggested I try writing romance. I thought he was crazy, but it was worth a try. That same night, I asked Melissa out, right there in the restaurant, and she actually said yes. I fell madly in love, I wrote my first romance, and the rest is history."

"Wow. Melissa was your muse?" Lisa asked.

"Yes, she was. Until she found a new guy and took half of everything I had. Actually, more than half because my lawyer sucked."

Lisa sat back in her chair. "That's quite a story. Who's your muse now?"

Avery gazed into her eyes and smiled warmly. "Guess."

Lisa's eyes widened as she figured out what he was suggesting. "No. Not me? You're just saying that to make me feel special."

He reached for her hand. "Would I lie?"

As she looked into his deep blue eyes, she could see he wasn't lying. "I'm flattered."

"You should be." He laughed. "It's a tough job, but I think you're up to the task."

She shook her head and laughed. He had a silly sense of humor and she liked that.

Avery paid the bill, despite her offering to pay half, and they drove back to her place. Tonight, she asked him if he'd like to come in for a drink. His eyes lit up and he accepted. Bailey was excited when they both entered, but he soon settled down. She poured them both a glass of red wine and they sat on the sofa. She kicked off her heels and sat back, relaxed after their nice evening of food and conversation. Avery sat down near her, taking her hand.

"So," he said, making a show of glancing around. "We're alone."

"It appears so," she said, grinning.

"And it seems to me there had been some talk about a kiss once. Was that today? Or yesterday?" He moved closer.

"I really don't remember," she teased.

"Can I refresh your memory?"

Lisa lifted her face to his as he moved even closer. Her stomach did a flip in anticipation of their kiss. Just as their lips were about to touch, there was a banging on her front door.

Bailey shot up and began barking.

Lisa startled, and the glass she'd been holding fell to the floor. Red wine spread over the tan and brown rug.

Avery sat back, looking frustrated. "Who in the world is that?"

Lisa hurried to the door and looked out the peephole. There stood Andrew holding a red-faced Abby. "It's Andrew and Abby," she told Avery as she unlocked the door.

Avery rolled his eyes, stood, and headed to the kitchen. "I'll get something for this stain," he said.

"Andrew. What's wrong?" Lisa was suddenly frightened by Abby's red, splotchy face. "Is she sick?"

Andrew walked inside as Lisa took Abby in her arms. Abby was crying, "Mommy! Mommy!"

"Mommy's here now, sweetie," Lisa cooed. "You're okay."

Andrew looked flustered. "I had to bring her back. She's been crying and upset for two days. We hardly slept at all last night."

From his mussed hair and the dark circles under his eyes, Lisa could tell he'd had a tough weekend. "What happened?" she asked.

"I don't know. She was fine when we got home on Friday. We went to a kid-friendly place for dinner and then she went to bed as usual. Suddenly, she was screaming and crying all night. She doesn't have a fever and she didn't throw up or anything, so I didn't know what was wrong. She just kept crying and asking for Bailey and Mommy." Andrew glanced over toward the sofa.

"Do you know your dog is licking something off the rug?"

"Crap!" Lisa hurried over to pull Bailey away from the wine stain while still balancing Abby on her hip.

"Baywee!" the little girl cried with glee.

Avery came out of the kitchen at that moment, carrying a handful of wet paper towels.

"What's he doing here?" Andrew asked, his faced creased with anger. "What is he now, your cleaner?"

Avery glared at Andrew but didn't say a word. He pulled Bailey away from the stain and started wiping it up.

"It's none of your business why Avery's here," Lisa snapped. "You were supposed to be at your own place with Abby."

Andrew folded his arms and stared at Lisa. "Well, she was having a bad weekend. I don't know why. Wouldn't you want me to bring her back here if I couldn't calm her down? I did the right thing."

Lisa nodded. Abby had already settled down and was yawning. The poor little girl was beat. "Yes. I'd rather you bring her home than have her cry the whole time. But I don't understand why she cried. Has she done this before?"

"She's cried, yeah. But Katrina usually finds a way to calm her down. I don't know what she does. She distracts her or something. Nothing worked for me."

Lisa was surprised that Katrina was the one who knew how to calm Abby down. She'd always seemed so disinterested in the little girl. "So, without Katrina's help, you can't take care of Abby?" she asked.

"I can. It was just a bad weekend, that's all," Andrew said, looking frustrated. He suddenly grew angry and pointed his finger at her. "And don't you try using this against me in court next week. This hasn't happened before. I did the right thing, bringing her back to you so she'd calm down."

Lisa didn't answer him because she couldn't be one-hundred percent certain she wouldn't mention this to her lawyer. If Abby was upset at his house all the time, what good would it be for her to be with him three or four days a week? Finally, she said, "Thank you for bringing her home. It looks like she's ready to fall asleep, so I'll put her to bed. Maybe your next weekend with her will be better."

"I hope so. This was rough." Andrew headed for the door, but before leaving, he scowled at Avery again. "Is this guy going to be here all the time now? If he is, I want to do a background check on him. I don't like strange men around my daughter."

Lisa was so stunned she couldn't get any words out of her mouth. Luckily, Avery beat her to it.

"Go ahead. Do a background check. The name's Avery McKinnon. I'm an author and I live across the street. I earn way more money than you do, and I don't have any debt. And I've also never been arrested. So, look all you want." He went back to blotting the stain on the rug.

Lisa held back a laugh. Andrew's face was bright red with anger, and he was clenching his hands into fists.

"There. Are you happy? Go home, Andrew. I have to put Abby to bed."

"Fine. I'm leaving. I'll see you in court on Wednesday." Andrew stormed out the door and Lisa shut and locked it.

"Good riddance," she said, making Avery chuckle. Then she took the already sleeping Abby to her room.

Chapter Sixteen

"Stupid jerk," Avery muttered as he poured a little more water on the wine stain then tried blotting it up. "How dare he question my integrity?"

Bailey came over and licked Avery's face, making him smile. "You trust me, and that's all that matters," he told the dog.

Lisa returned from tucking Abby into bed. "She's sound asleep. There's nothing wrong with her that I can tell except she missed her mommy and her dog."

"I don't blame her," Avery said. "I'd miss you too." Lisa smiled warmly and Avery's heart did a little flip. How many times had he nearly kissed her and been interrupted? It was almost becoming comical. Almost.

"That stain looks like it isn't coming out," Lisa said, studying it. "I'll have to see if I have any carpet cleaner that will work. Thanks for trying, though."

"I didn't want Bailey to lick it all up. No one needs a drunk dog."

She laughed. "I guess this night didn't turn out exactly as we'd hoped. But I'm glad he brought her home. I'd hate to think of Abby crying all weekend."

"I agree. That would be sad," Avery said. He drew nearer

to Lisa. "We were this close." He had his finger and thumb less than an inch apart.

She grinned. "We'll get there. Someday. But I'm afraid I'll have to call it a night. Mornings come early when Abby's home."

Avery sighed. "Okay. I understand." He wrapped his arms around her and kissed her forehead. "Next time, I'm not going to plan it. I'm just going to grab you and kiss you, so we don't get interrupted. Can I have your permission to do that?"

"Permission granted," she said. "Surprise me."

He waggled his brows and made her laugh again. He loved making her laugh.

As he headed for the door, he asked, "Do you want me to drive you to your court date on Wednesday? I'd be happy to."

Slowly, she shook her head. "Thanks, but no. It would be very easy for me to lean on you during that, but I need to stand on my own two feet. I'll just have to accept whatever happens."

"Okay." He stepped outside the door as Lisa stood inside. "I really hate to leave."

"I hate for you to leave, too," she whispered. "Go home. Write. Maybe I'll see you tomorrow?"

"Try and keep me away," he said.

Once at home, Avery changed into his sweats and sat down at his computer. It was already eleven o'clock, but he didn't care. He could get a couple of thousand words done before heading to bed.

However, his mind kept returning to Lisa and how they'd almost kissed tonight. She'd been so relaxed and happy, the most relaxed he'd ever seen her. He was glad they'd had a chance to talk about their pasts. He really wanted to get to know her better—not just physically—as if that were an option. He chuckled to himself. The universe seemed to be against them kissing. Maybe it was a sign. He hoped not. He really liked Lisa and he already adored Abby. And Bailey. The dog that had driven him crazy had found a way into his heart. It was amazing how people could change. How he had changed, from angry at the world to hopeful again.

As he read over the words he'd written previously, he realized that his writing had changed, as well. His happiness was showing in the manuscript, and that made the story so much better.

Avery spent Sunday with Lisa, Abby, and Bailey, going for a walk in the park as Lisa pulled Abby in her wagon. The weather was beautiful—high sixties with the sun shining. They took advantage of the nice autumn day. He ate dinner at their house then went back home to write some more. He was on a roll with the story, so he didn't want to spend too much time away from his computer. Melissa used to complain about all the time he'd spent writing. But Lisa encouraged him to write. The two women were such opposites—night and day. Lisa brought out the good in him that he hadn't known still existed. His joy was making him write better than he'd ever written before.

On Monday night, as Avery was working until the early morning hours, he stopped typing. He realized he was now at the pivotal scene of the romance, but he wasn't sure which direction this story would go. He knew how he wanted it to end but couldn't figure out how he was going to get the characters to the ending he envisioned.

Avery sat back in his chair and sighed. He was so close, yet he felt his goal was still far out of reach.

Am I thinking about the book, or Lisa?

He wasn't sure. He couldn't get Lisa off his mind while he was writing. But, to be fair, he was using Lisa as the model for his character so that made it even harder not to think about her. It was so odd. A month ago, he'd only known Lisa as the lady with the annoying dog. Now, he was falling for her. Could a person really fall head over heels in love in one month? That only happened in romance novels.

Or in real life if you're lucky.

Avery still had a little more time to finish this novel, so he could afford to wait for the story to come to him. He'd work it out in his head, little by little. But he had a feeling that the end would be tied to how things worked out with Lisa. He hoped that both had a happy ending.

* * *

Wednesday came quickly for Lisa. She went to work as usual but had brought along a change of clothes for later in the day. She took off from work at one-thirty and drove to the courthouse. Sitting in her car, staring up at the large building, she grew nervous. What if the judge granted Andrew joint custody and lowered her child support payments? Could she afford to keep her house? She was already pinching pennies as tightly as she could. She saw no way to squeeze any more money from her earnings or even earn extra income. The money issue scared her. The thought of Andrew having Abby with him three or four days a week bothered her too. If he insisted on her living half-time with him, how would they manage it? And how would that disrupt Abby's life? Lisa couldn't imagine a young child being bounced around from house to house every week. She knew parents did it, but Lisa wasn't sure if she could.

All of this was tearing at her nerves.

Her lawyer, Ben Jankowski, pulled up in the parking space beside her. Lisa got out and they walked together up the stairs and into the building.

"You look worried. Try to relax," Ben told her. He smiled, and she calmed down a little. Ben was in his early forties with dark hair that was graying slightly at the temples. He was a high-energy person who ran five miles a day and not only worked in his own law firm but also took on several pro bono cases every month. He'd helped Lisa with her divorce, and she trusted him to do the best he could with this new custody battle.

"I know the judge is going to see right through Andrew," Ben said. "Your husband didn't fight for full or joint custody when you divorced, so it's obvious it's about the money now. Judges don't like that."

Lisa nodded. She hoped that was true.

Ben led her to Judge Kenrich's outer office where they were told to take a seat and wait.

Five minutes later, Andrew came in with his lawyer, Constance Randall, a tall woman in her fifties who didn't let anyone push her around. Everyone nodded to each other without saying a word. Lisa noticed that Andrew looked worried too. She had no idea why. He was the one who'd started this new custody battle. He must have realized there was a chance he might not win after all.

They were finally allowed to enter the judge's chambers. Judge Kenrich sat behind his desk, a pair of half-moon glasses sitting on the end of his nose. He rose when the women entered then sat after they had. Old fashioned manners, Lisa thought. She liked that.

They all waited in silence until the judge spoke. "I've read over your file and I have a few questions." He peered over his glasses at Andrew. "Mr. Evans. Would you explain why you didn't ask for joint custody at the time of the divorce and why you suddenly want it now?"

Andrew cleared his throat. Lisa knew he could be confident and charming at times like these, but today he looked unsure. "When we divorced, I hadn't thought through the custody issue thoroughly, Your Honor. And I wasn't settled in my townhouse and felt it would be best not to disrupt my daughter's life any more than necessary. Now, however, I'm settled in a nice place and have a room set up for her. I feel that I should spend more time with my daughter."

"Hmm," the judge said. "Do you live alone, Mr. Evans?"

Andrew frowned and glanced at his lawyer for direction. She nodded, as if to tell him it was okay to answer. "Yes, sir. I currently live alone."

Lisa's brows shot up. Did that mean Katrina had moved out?

The judge spoke again. "I understand your daughter was recently in the hospital overnight. It says here that Mrs. Evans was unable to reach you the entire weekend. Do you generally turn off your phone?"

Andrew glared at Lisa, but she sat tall and held her ground. He was the one who filed against her, so she was going to use whatever it took to win the case.

"No, sir," Andrew answered. "I don't make a habit of turning off my phone. I am almost always available 24/7 for Lisa to call me. I explained to her that it wouldn't happen again."

"I see." The judge turned his gaze to Lisa. "Mrs. Evans. How do you feel about sharing custody with your husband?"

She took a breath to calm herself then answered, "Your Honor, Andrew knows that he can see our daughter any time he wishes. I've never kept her away from him. As for sharing custody, I honestly feel that Abby's too young to be moved between households every few days. The day care she attends is next door to the school I work at, so it's convenient for me to have her during the week. Andrew would have to drive out of his way to bring her there. Maybe it could be an option when she's older, but for now, I'm afraid it would only confuse her. If Andrew wants to take her to dinner or spend time with her during the week, he's more than welcome to do so."

The judge nodded at her, looked down at the papers once more, then sat up straighter in his chair. "Considering the fact that Mr. Evans didn't ask for custody at the time of the divorce, and that the child is doing well at home with Mrs. Evans, I agree that she is too young to have her life disrupted by being moved between houses at this time. We can re-open this discussion in a year, if the father still wishes to pursue this issue. Otherwise, the custody will remain the same as will the child support payments."

Lisa let out a sigh of relief as her lawyer smiled over at her.

Andrew stared at his attorney, but she didn't say anything. She gathered her papers into her briefcase as if accepting the judge's decision without question.

The judge excused himself and the foursome headed out of the offices and into the hallway. Andrew immediately cornered Lisa.

"I can't believe you used that weekend Abby was sick against me. You know damn well I'd never purposely ignore calls from you about Abby. I called you the moment I saw the messages."

"Yes, you did. But by then it was too late. Besides, you know you only wanted shared custody so you could lower child support payments. I know you wouldn't take Abby half the time. You never call during the week to ask to see her."

Andrew's lips formed a thin line. "Well, you got what you wanted. I hope you're happy." He turned and stormed down the hallway, ignoring his lawyer as she followed him.

"Are you okay?" Ben asked her. He'd stood nearby just in

case Andrew got out of control.

"I'm fine. Thank you so much for all you've done. At least I have another year before I have to worry about him petitioning the court again."

"Call me if he does. You know where to find me."

He walked her to her car and Lisa drove back to the school to pick Abby up from day care. She was so relieved. She was pretty sure that after Andrew had given it some thought, he'd realize the judge had made the right decision. No matter what, she'd try her best not to give him a reason to go after Abby again.

That evening after Lisa had fed Abby her dinner and put her to bed, Avery texted her.

How did it go in court today?

She smiled. It was nice that he cared enough to ask. *The judge ruled in my favor,* she texted back. *At least for another year. I'm hoping that Andrew doesn't file again after that.*

Congrats! I have wine. Do you want me to bring it over for a little celebration?

Lol. Thanks, but I should go to bed early. I hardly slept at all last night. Can I have a raincheck?

Sure, he texted. *Let's see. That's one raincheck for wine and one for a kiss. You owe me, lady!* ☺

She laughed. *You just keep track and we'll see.*

Goodnight.

Goodnight, she texted. She smiled the whole time she turned out the lights and headed off to bed.

Chapter Seventeen

Avery loved his life. It felt good to once again belong somewhere and be around people who cared about him. If he could just get Maddie back, everything would be perfect.

And maybe buy his former home. But that might be asking for too much.

Avery worked on his book all week and late Friday night, as he sat at his computer, he was surprised to see snow falling. An early October snow wasn't unusual for Minnesota, but it wasn't the norm, either. By morning when he'd awoken, it was piled high everywhere. Everyone in the neighborhood was out shoveling their driveways and sidewalks, Lisa included. He dressed quickly and headed across the street, his shovel in hand.

"Isn't this crazy?" Lisa asked as he drew near. Abby was bundled up in her coat and snow pants and sat on the porch with Bailey, the latter wagging his tail happily at the sight of Avery.

"It is," Avery agreed. "But at least it isn't too cold out." He began shoveling out her driveway while she did the sidewalk. Afterward, she offered to heat up soup and make grilled cheese sandwiches for lunch. By mid-afternoon, the sun was shining, so the three of them went out into the front yard and began building a snowman. Avery started a small ball and had Abby help him push it around until it became bigger, with Bailey bounding around behind them. Abby laughed happily as they both slipped and fell in the snow. Soon they had three balls that Avery stacked to make a snowman. Lisa brought out buttons and a carrot for the face and Avery lifted the little girl so she could help place them. A scarf and a stocking cap Lisa found in the closet were the finishing touches. Already, the snow around them was melting, but the snowman was sure to survive at least a couple of days.

Kristen and Marie had also made a snowman in their yard and Kristen brought over a thermos of hot chocolate that they all shared on Lisa's front porch. The little girls ran around Abby's snowman, and Bailey and Sam followed. It was a happy day, a sweet memory, and Avery took a photo of the two little girls in front of the snowman so he could remember this.

That evening, Avery ordered pizza and the three of them ate hungrily after all their outside activity. Abby's eyes grew heavy and Lisa put her to bed where she fell asleep immediately. Coming out of Abby's room, Lisa dropped down on the sofa next to Avery, who'd just poured her a glass of red wine. She looked at him with a sparkle in her eyes.

"What?" he asked. "Is there something wrong with me?"

She laughed and shook her head. "No. There's nothing wrong with you. In fact, you amaze me. You're the real deal, aren't you?"

His brows shot up. "The real deal?"

"Yes. Some men are nice to a woman's child to get to her. But you really had fun today. You were so good with Abby. And you've been great with Bailey. You're a good guy. The real deal." She grinned. "That is, for a hermit."

He laughed and reached his arm around her, pulling her

close. "Hermits need love too," he said. She laughed, and as he looked into her eyes, he thought how much he enjoyed her laugh and her smile. Making Lisa happy made him happy. He hadn't felt this good in a long time. He didn't have to wait for the right moment. This was the right moment. He pulled her to him and kissed her, just as he'd said he would. It was a soft, gentle kiss, and when he pulled away a moment, he saw her blue eyes twinkle and he wanted to kiss her some more. He could kiss her all night, and it wouldn't be enough. Their lips met again, this time opening for a deeper kiss as his hand ran through her silky hair.

Heaven, he thought. *This is what heaven feels like.*

Her phone rang at that moment and she pulled away, looking stunned.

"You've got to be kidding me," he said, disappointed.

She glanced at it and frowned. "It's the hospital."

"Hospital? Who could be there?"

She sat back on the sofa. "I don't know, but I should answer it."

Avery nodded reluctantly. "Yes. You should."

She answered the call and after talking for a couple of minutes, and asking questions, she hung up. "It's Andrew. Apparently, he slipped on the ice and broke his leg."

"Are you kidding me?" Avery asked. "Why did they call you?"

She shrugged. "I guess there's no one else for him to call. I'm still listed as his emergency contact. He's at the emergency room right now. They need me to go there. She said something about surgery." Lisa stood. "I'm sorry, Avery. I'd better go. I don't know how badly he's hurt."

Avery stood and wrapped his arms around her, enjoying the feel of her body next to his. She hugged him back, in no hurry to separate. "I can drive you," he offered.

She pulled back. "I'd rather not wake Abby and drag her there. Would you mind staying here with her? She should sleep the entire time."

Avery nodded. Lisa was right. It would be silly to wake Abby this late at night. "Sure."

Lisa placed a sweet kiss on his lips. "Thank you. As usual, you're a lifesaver."

He grinned and held her tight. "Are you sure you want to go see him when you could be here, safe and warm, with me?"

"Honestly, I'd prefer staying here with you. But I'd better go. He has no one else."

"Okay," Avery said, disappointed. All he could think, though, was that Andrew didn't deserve to have Lisa come to his aid. He didn't deserve her at all.

* * *

Forty-five minutes later, Lisa was led to a room in the emergency department where Andrew was lying on a bed, his leg straight out in front of him. By the look of his pupils, he was on some heavy-duty pain killers.

"There she is," he said cheerfully to the female nurse standing on the other side of the bed. "I knew she'd come."

Lisa wanted to roll her eyes but refrained. Did she have a choice except to come? "How's your leg?" she asked Andrew.

"Broken," he said, a deadpan look on his face. Then he grinned. "Really broken. But I don't feel a thing after what they've given me."

"Are you his wife?" the nurse asked.

"No. I'm the ex-wife. But I was on his form as the person to call."

"Oh. Okay. I'll tell the doctor you're here and she can explain what's going on." She walked out a door on the opposite side from where Lisa had entered.

Lisa turned to Andrew. "How did you break your leg?"

He frowned. "It was a stupid accident. I'd gone into work this afternoon because the system was acting up and they needed it working properly before Monday. I was lucky enough to find a parking space right outside the building, and since it was a Saturday, I wouldn't get a ticket. But the plow must have come through while I was inside, and snow was piled up next to my car on the driver's side. I came out later in the evening and I thought it was just wet snow, but it had iced up once the sun went down. When I stepped on it to get into the car, I fell and slipped halfway under the car. I was lucky I didn't get run over."

Lisa winced. "That's terrible. What part of your leg is broken?"

Before Andrew could answer, the doctor joined them and, showing them the x-rays, explained that he'd cracked his thigh bone in two places and would need surgery to add screws before putting on a cast.

Lisa couldn't believe the damage he'd done to his leg just by falling, but Andrew was so drugged that he didn't seem too worried about it. "When will you operate?" she asked.

"We'll admit him tonight and operate in the morning. He'll have to stay a couple of days. Once he has a cast on, he can go home," the doctor said. "But we'll need someone to fill out the paperwork and sign a release form."

"Why can't he sign it?" Lisa asked.

"We need someone who isn't drugged and understands what it says. He's been given morphine for the pain, so that's why you were called in."

"Okay. Fine," Lisa said. After the doctor left, she said to Andrew. "Do you understand what's going on here? They're going to operate tomorrow, and you'll be in a cast for a while."

"Yep. I get it," he said, sounding half loopy.

"So you're okay with me signing the papers for you to go into surgery?"

"Yep."

Lisa slumped down in the plastic chair by the wall. "Are you and Katrina completely over? Or should I call her?"

Andrew let out a big snort of laughter. "Over! Caput! Finished!"

"I guess that's a yes," she said.

Andrew's eyes were getting heavy. "Absolutely yes," he said. He shut his eyes and looked like he'd fallen into a deep sleep.

The nurse came in and handed Lisa the paperwork. Lisa nodded toward Andrew. "He's out. How much morphine has he had?"

"He was in excruciating pain when the ambulance brought him in," the nurse said. "I think that wore him out and the morphine helped to finally relax him. It's good he's sleeping. He'll need his rest before surgery tomorrow."

Lisa nodded. She filled out his paperwork, signed the consent form, and waited until he was settled into a room before going home. She'd decided she'd be back at the hospital tomorrow during his surgery just to make sure everything went fine. After that, he'd be on his own.

When she arrived home, she found Avery sound asleep on her sofa. He'd kicked off his shoes and had lain back on one of the pillows. He looked so comfortable, she didn't have the heart to wake him. Lisa took the throw blanket off the back of the sofa and gently spread it over him, then placed a light kiss on his cheek. "Goodnight, hermit," she said softly. She turned out the light and headed to bed.

* * *

Lisa and Abby were already eating an early breakfast by the time Avery awoke. "Hey, sleepyhead," Lisa called from the dining room table.

He sat up on the couch and smiled when he saw them. "What time is it?"

"Seven."

"Seven? Do you usually get up this early on the weekend?"

Lisa laughed. "Sometimes, but not generally. I have to be at the hospital by eight for Andrew's surgery. Kristen is going to watch Abby while I'm gone."

"Surgery? What did I miss?" Avery made his way to the table with Bailey at his heels.

Lisa explained what had happened to Andrew as Avery poured a mug of coffee and sat down with them.

"That sounds terrible," he said, wincing. "If you give me a few minutes, I'll go home and change, and I can drive you there. You don't want to sit alone and wait."

She smiled. "Thanks. I'll take you up on that. I hate hospitals."

He chuckled. "That coming from a nurse."

She grinned. "You know what I mean, silly."

They left a half hour later. The day had warmed considerably from the previous one and the sun shone brightly. Almost all the snow was gone. "Hopefully we won't get snow again for at least another month," Avery said. "But you never know."

When they arrived at the hospital, Lisa learned that Andrew was already in surgery. She asked to be notified when he was done, then sat down in the waiting room with Avery. The room was large and decorated in green and brown, which Lisa figured they'd done to make it feel soothing. But waiting in a hospital, no matter what the color scheme, was never soothing. It was always nerve-wracking.

"Are you nervous?" Andrew asked.

"No. I'm sure Andrew will be fine. This is a good hospital. I was just thinking of the night we brought in Abby. Waiting for news is difficult."

He took her hand and squeezed it. "Then I'm doubly glad that I came along."

She smiled over at him. "Me, too."

"So, I had my first sleepover at your place. Was it as good for you as it was for me?" He winked.

Lisa laughed, then placed a hand over her mouth to stifle it. "You're terrible," she said.

He waggled his brows, which only made her laugh harder. She loved how he could lighten the mood when she was feeling tense.

"Last night didn't exactly play out the way we'd planned," she said. "But at least you finally got that first kiss."

Avery grinned. "That's right. I'm looking forward to the second, and third, and many, many more."

She leaned over toward him and whispered, "I am too."

They sat there, holding hands, for over two hours until a nurse came out and reported that all had gone well, and Andrew was doing fine.

"He's very groggy right now," the nurse told her. "He'll be that way for the rest of the day with the pain killers we're giving him. It would probably be best to come back later this afternoon if you'd like to see him."

Lisa thanked her and the nurse walked away. "We might as

well go home," Lisa said. "There's no sense sitting around here."

"You're the boss," Avery said. They drove back to her place and she went next door to pick up Abby.

They ate lunch together then Avery suggested they all take a walk since the weather was nice. Lisa loaded Abby in her wagon and Avery put Bailey on his leash. They took off down the street, looking like a sweet little family. Once at the park, they stopped at the swing set for a while and Lisa pushed Abby in a toddler-friendly swing. The little girl giggled with glee each time the swing went up in the air and fell back. Avery sat on a bench with Bailey sitting by his side. After a while, Lisa and Abby joined him on the bench.

"This is nice," Avery said, placing his arm around her shoulders. "I could do this all the time and never tire of it."

Lisa turned to him and smiled. "I could get used to it."

After the walk home, Avery offered to drive Lisa back to the hospital, and he could keep Abby with him while Lisa checked on Andrew. "Then we can go out for dinner," he said.

She agreed, and they tucked Abby into her car seat and headed back to the hospital.

Lisa quietly walked into Andrew's room in case he was sleeping. He had a private room, and it was actually quite big. She found him lying in bed, his leg bandaged and stretched out in front of him. He looked glassy-eyed, and there were dark circles under his eyes.

"Hey there," he said when he saw her.

"Hi. How are you feeling?"

"Like I was hit by a truck. I feel so tired, but at least I'm not in pain."

"That's good. You must be on some high-powered pain killers again," Lisa said.

He nodded. He looked so worn out that she didn't want to stay long and tire him more.

"I just wanted to check on you. I was here this morning during your surgery and the nurse came out to tell us you were fine."

"You were here?" he asked, looking surprised. "That was nice of you. Thank you."

"I'm sure you would have done the same for me," she said, not really certain if that was the truth.

"I'd like to think I would have," he answered. "I appreciate you caring enough to come. Is Abby with you?" He glanced around, looking confused, like maybe he just hadn't seen his daughter come in.

"She's waiting downstairs with Avery. I thought it might scare her to see you this way."

He frowned. "Avery? The gardener?"

She shook her head. "I guess no amount of drugs will soften your attitude."

This actually made him smile. "Sorry."

She changed the subject. "Do they know when they'll be putting on the cast?"

"I think they said the day after tomorrow, depending on how fast the swelling goes down. Then I have to stay another day before they'll release me."

"That's a long time," she said.

He agreed. "Can I ask you a big favor?"

"Okay," she said warily.

"Would you stop by my place and pick up a few personal items for me? Like a change of clothes—probably jogging pants that zip open on the sides—and my razor and toothbrush. I literally have nothing here."

"I can do that, sure," she said. "Can I take your keys?"

He nodded. His eyelids were getting droopy and she could tell he was fighting to stay awake. "They're in the nightstand drawer."

She took them out and dropped them in her purse. "I'll see you tomorrow after work," she said.

Andrew didn't answer. He'd already fallen into a deep sleep.

"Goodnight," she said softly, then turned and left the room.

Chapter Eighteen

Avery took Lisa and Abby to a family-friendly restaurant to eat. Afterward, they stopped by Andrew's townhouse to pick up his things. Avery drove through the upscale community of brand-new townhouses, searching for Andrew's section. There was a large park for children to play and a huge pool for the residents. He also noticed there were tennis courts and figured there was probably a private gym somewhere on the property too. He finally found Andrew's parking space—number 209— and pulled into it.

As they entered the townhouse, he glanced around. It was two levels with the kitchen, living and dining rooms, and a bathroom on the main level. He followed Lisa upstairs where there were three bedrooms—Andrew's large master bedroom and bathroom, Abby's room, and another room that was used as an office. A third bathroom was also upstairs.

"He certainly isn't pinching pennies with this place, is he?" Avery said quietly to Lisa. It angered him that Andrew wanted to lower his support for Abby while he lived in a place as luxurious as this.

"He called it an investment," she said, rolling her eyes. "I think he believed he and Katrina would be together for the long haul and their two incomes would pay for it."

"He should have been more careful with his money," Avery said.

Abby grabbed Avery's hand. "My ruum," she said, pulling on him.

He smiled down at her. "Let's go see your room."

Abby led him into her room which was fit for a princess. There was a toddler bed with railings and a filmy pink curtain hung from the ceiling, draped over it like a fancy tent. A pink bedspread with a Disney princess was covered in decorative pillows and fluffy stuffed animals. The white dresser held a musical carousal, and a toy box on the other wall was filled to the brim with toys. Another shelf was full of children's books. Avery had to admit that Andrew wasn't cheap when it came to his daughter.

Abby pulled a white stuffed bear off the bed that looked like it had been hugged and loved a lot. "Snowfrake," she said proudly, hugging the bear.

"Snowflake. That's a great name for a polar bear," Avery said.

Abby walked over to the toybox and began pulling out her favorite toys. It seemed as if every one lit up or played music. She sat on the floor next to Avery and began playing with the toys, handing him one then another for him to play with too. He smiled at how cute she was. She was sharing her favorite toys with him, and he knew that was special.

"Are you two having fun?" Lisa asked a few minutes later as she poked her head into the room.

"Of course," Avery said. "I've learned a lot of new songs. One for counting, one for colors, and one for animals."

Lisa chuckled. "You can never know too many songs." She knelt beside Abby. "Come on, honey. Time to pick up the toys and go home." When Abby protested, Lisa made a game of putting the toys back in the box and Abby cheered up and happily played along. She couldn't talk her out of letting the bear stay there, though, and gave in and let Abby bring it with her.

"You have to choose your battles," Lisa told Avery. Avery thought she'd chosen well. He liked how patient Lisa was with Abby. She was definitely a good mother.

Later, after he'd brought them home and Lisa had put Abby to bed, the two sat on the sofa as Bailey snoozed in the hallway, protecting Abby.

"Thanks for bringing me to Andrew's tonight. You're so good with Abby. I'm surprised you've never had children," Lisa said.

"Melissa isn't the motherly type," Avery said. "And I never really thought about it one way or another. Now, I wouldn't mind having children. Abby is so adorable. It's easy being around her. And you're amazing with her."

"Well, I've had practice," she said.

"Do you think you'll want more children someday?"

Lisa shrugged. "It depends on if and when I meet someone I'd want to have children with. I'm thirty-two now. I only have a few more years where I'd still want to have children."

"You're so old," he said, grinning.

She hit him lightly. "And how old are you?"

"Thirty-six. But men don't have an expiration date on having children. I could be a father when I'm in my sixties."

"Ugh! Not me! My sixties will be for retiring, traveling, and sleeping in!"

Avery laughed. He wrapped his arm around her, and she laid her head on his shoulder. He liked having her close to him. Her hair smelled of strawberry shampoo and the skin of her arm felt soft as he lightly brushed it with his fingertips. "Where would you like to travel?"

"I want to go to the Bahamas and lie on a sandy beach as the tide rolls in. I want to go to Paris and spend all day at the Louvre and go up to the top of the Eiffel Tower. I want to go to London and Italy, and travel by car all over the United States and see everything."

"That all sounds amazing," Avery said softly as he kissed the top of her head. "Can I go with you?"

Lisa nodded. "Sure. Why not?"

She sounded sleepy and Avery just sat quietly and stroked her hair until he heard the slow rhythmic breathing of sleep. He kissed her again and whispered, "I'll take you anywhere you want to go." Then he laid his head on hers and held her a while longer.

* * *

On Wednesday, Lisa stopped by the hospital to check on Andrew. She'd dropped Abby off at Kristen's before going because she wanted it to be a quick trip. He'd asked her to bring a couple more things he needed, and she planned to drop them off and leave. Avery was grilling hamburgers at her house for dinner that night and she was in a hurry to get home and relax.

When she entered Andrew's room, she was surprised to see he had a cast on his leg.

"This is new," she said, and he smiled up at her. He looked much better after a few days of rest.

"They put it on this afternoon. I'm told that if all looks well, I can leave tomorrow."

She set his things on the table by his bed. "I'll bet you're ready to leave and go home."

"I am, but…" He paused.

Lisa frowned. "But what?"

"I can't get around on my own for a couple of weeks until they put a walking cast on. I'll be limited in what I can do. They suggested I ask a friend or relative to let me stay with them for at least a couple of weeks." He looked at her hopefully.

It took a moment for his words to sink in. Lisa eyed him warily. "What exactly are you saying?"

"I was wondering if you'd let me stay with you at the house. I could sleep in the den downstairs. All the bedrooms in my place are upstairs."

She shook her head vehemently. "No. Absolutely not. You can sleep on your sofa for all I care."

"But I'll need help. And someone to cook for me and help me get around."

"Ask Katrina to come stay with you for a while. Or hire a nurse," Lisa said.

"You are a nurse."

"I don't care," Lisa said, growing angrier. "I work all day and I have Abby to take care of. I'm not taking care of you, too, and you're definitely not living in my house."

"It was my house once too," he argued.

"Not anymore. You have your own place. I'm not responsible for you anymore." She stood there with her arms crossed in front of her, unyielding. She could tell by the look on Andrew's face that he was trying to think of a way to get her to say yes. *There's no way in hell,* she thought.

"I'll make you a deal," he said, sounding calmer. "If you let me stay at the house for a couple of weeks, and you help me, I'll give up pursuing joint custody and I'll continue to pay the full child support without a complaint."

She stared at him as she contemplated his words. "You can't pursue custody for another year anyway and you're legally required to pay child support. So how do you think this would benefit me?"

Andrew ran his hand through his hair, looking frustrated. "I promise I won't pursue it in a year, or two years, or ever. And I won't complain about child support or how it's spent ever again. Lisa, I need your help. I don't like having to ask, but at least I'm offering you something in return. Please. I don't have anyone else to turn to right now."

Lisa took a deep breath and turned to stare out the window. He seemed sincere about his offer, and she knew it hadn't been easy for Andrew to beg her for help. But she also knew that his staying at her house was going to be difficult.

And what about Avery? They were just starting to get close. How could she keep seeing him if Andrew was around every corner? But she had to think of Abby first. If Andrew truly meant what he'd said, she'd never have to worry about him paying her less for support when she so desperately needed the money.

Finally, she faced him. "Two weeks. That's it."

Andrew exhaled loudly. "Thank you."

"But I want it in writing that you will no longer pursue joint custody and will pay support without complaint," Lisa said.

"Fine. I'll write it up and sign it. I really appreciate this, Lisa. I know it'll be difficult, and I'll try not to drive you crazy." He smiled.

"You already are driving me crazy," she said. *And ruining my social life, what little there is.*

"It might be fun," he offered. "I'll get to spend more time with Abby, and we can hang out like we used to. Maybe we can do some binge watching on Netflix together."

Lisa sighed. It was *not* going to be fun. It was going to mean extra work for her, and she already knew that he was going to annoy her. But she was doing this for Abby. And she'd do anything for her little girl.

She just had to think of how she was going to explain this to Avery.

* * *

"What?" Avery stared at her in disbelief.

"I told Andrew I'd let him stay here for two weeks until he could get around better by himself," she said again.

"Why would you do that? You don't owe him anything. He has a nice house of his own he can go to."

"He can't be alone right now," Lisa explained. "He can barely move around without help and he's on pain killers. It isn't safe for him to be alone while he takes those."

Avery couldn't believe what he was hearing. Her ex-husband wanted to move in? That sounded crazy. "I don't see how you can take care of him. You work all day. What's he going to do while you're gone?"

"He called Kristen and asked if she'd check on him during the day and make him lunch. His insurance will pay her to do that. I'll help him the rest of the time."

"I hope he's paying you too," Avery said.

Lisa sighed. "No, he's not. I made a better deal with him. One that will keep Abby with me permanently."

"What deal is that?"

"He said he wouldn't pursue joint custody and lower his child support payments—ever. He even put it in writing. I just have to put up with him for two weeks and I'll no longer have to worry that I won't get enough money to help support Abby until she's in college. It's a fair trade."

Avery stepped closer and placed his hands gently on her arms. "He's blackmailing you, Lisa. He's bribing you to do what he wants in exchange for something he should do anyway."

She turned and walked away from him, her arms crossed. They'd had a nice dinner and he'd played with Abby and Bailey outdoors until it grew chilly. She'd held out all evening from telling him what she'd agreed to because she knew he would react this way. But he didn't understand. How could he?

"Lisa?"

"You don't realize how important his payments are to me, and to Abby's well-being. Without them, we'd have to let go of this house. Where would we go? I love this neighborhood. It's the perfect place to raise Abby. I need to ensure he'll keep making those payments."

"You're going to let him manipulate you? So he can get what he wants?"

Anger welled up inside her. She felt cornered by Andrew, and now by Avery. Lisa spun around and faced him. "Yes. I'm going to let him manipulate me. But who are you to talk? You let Melissa manipulate you. She's blackmailing you for more money so you can get Maddie back."

Avery's expression darkened. "Yeah, but the difference is, I didn't give in to her."

"That's because you don't have to," Lisa's voice rose. "The stakes aren't as high for you as they are for me. This is about my daughter. This is about making a good life for her. You have enough money to live any way you want. You have the money to live wherever you want and however you want. All you need to do is sell another book to buy your precious mansion back. I need to support my daughter as best as I can. I have no options." Tears fell down her cheeks and she swiped them away. She hated that he was seeing her cry. She had to be strong. She always had to be strong—for Abby.

Avery looked stunned. "So, that's what you think of me? That I'm some spoiled rich guy just slumming it here for a while and I'll leave when I get bored?"

Lisa didn't think that, but she was too angry to answer. He'd already made her feel bad for the choice she'd made, and she couldn't afford to feel bad about it. She had to do what was necessary.

"Fine," Avery said. He grabbed his jacket off the back of the rocker and headed for the door. "I'm sorry I messed up your life. I'll leave you alone." He headed out the door, shutting it behind him.

The tears began to fall faster. Lisa fell on the sofa and dropped her head in her hands. Bailey came to her, placing his head near hers. She reached out, hugged him, and cried into his fur.

Chapter Nineteen

Avery stormed across the street, entered the house, and slammed his door. The entire wall rattled, but he didn't care. He was so angry he could break something. Anything. Instead, he crossed through the living room to the kitchen, grabbed a beer from the fridge, and guzzled it down.

He sat on a stool at the counter and looked around the house. In the past month since he'd met Lisa, he'd spent very little time here except to write. Almost every evening had been spent with Lisa and Abby, going to dinner, eating at her house, or taking long walks to the park. Many afternoons he'd gone to get Bailey while Lisa was at work and trained the dog to heel. One month. That was all it had been. Yet, it had felt like a lifetime. A wonderful lifetime. Lisa and Abby and Bailey had given him his life back. They'd given him a reason to be happy again. Now, it was over.

"That was probably Andrew's plan all along," he muttered to himself. "He's trying to work his way back into her life, and just watch. He'll do it."

Avery hadn't been this furious in a long time. Not when Melissa left him. Not even when Melissa took half of his money. He'd been angry about losing Maddie, and still was, but this was even worse. Losing Lisa was definitely much worse.

Suddenly, his shoulders slumped, and his heart ached. He thought about going back over there and apologizing for what he'd said. But would she listen? He'd still be upset over Andrew manipulating her. And once Andrew moved in, it would be hard to be civil to him, knowing what a jerk he was.

No, it was better if he left things alone.

Defeated, Avery changed into sweats and went to his office. He flipped open his laptop and waited for it to start up. He'd had an email from his agent this morning saying he'd loved the first five chapters that Avery had sent him. "Hurry with the rest," he'd written. The problem was, Avery didn't get the ending he'd hoped for. The happily-ever-after he'd hoped both he and his characters might have.

With a heavy heart, he began typing, trying his best to write a happy ending despite how broken he felt.

* * *

Two days later, Lisa picked Andrew up from the hospital after work and drove him to her house. She'd left Abby with Kristen because Andrew required the entire back seat to rest his leg on. The car was loaded with things he'd need, a set of crutches, a folded-up wheelchair, just in case, and a suitcase she'd packed for him at his house the night before.

Ryan was home from work, so he came over the minute they drove up and helped Andrew out of the car and into the house. He settled him on the sofa, then helped Lisa carry in the rest of the items.

"Thanks, Ryan," Lisa said. She hadn't known how she'd get Andrew into the house. She was so thankful for her neighbors.

"No problem," he said. He headed back inside to see if he could help Andrew with anything else.

As she returned to the car to get the last of Andrew's things, she saw Avery, wearing a heavy sweatshirt, walking on the opposite sidewalk at a brisk pace with his head down. She knew he was going for his daily walk, but without Bailey. She sighed. They hadn't spoken since their fight, neither of them making the effort to reach out first. She'd had a moment of weakness the day after, and her finger had hovered over his number on her phone, but then she'd decided against it. He'd been angry when he'd left. And she'd been angry too. Maybe they'd said things they couldn't apologize for. Besides, with Andrew here, it would only be more complicated trying to see Avery. Maybe it was for the best. Yet, she missed him. Sadly, she'd always wonder what could have been.

The next few days went by in a blur. Every morning was a rush, making breakfast for Andrew, helping him dress and use the bathroom before heading out with Abby to work and day care. The evenings were just as busy: making dinner, Abby's bath time, Andrew's shower with one leg out of the tub, (which was awkward to say the least), and getting them both settled into bed before she fell, exhausted, into her own. She knew Andrew was trying to be a good patient, and he did play with Abby as much as possible. But he always had the television on, which annoyed Lisa, and he was always asking for water, a soda, or a snack. She'd forgotten how much he ate. But the worst thing was his constant complaining about Bailey.

"Get out of my face!" he'd yell at the dog. "Get away from the television! Can't this stupid dog go outside?"

Lisa ignored Andrew as much as possible, but when she'd get annoyed, she'd remind him who'd bought the dog in the first place.

"I can see it was a big mistake," he'd blurted out, which only angered Lisa more.

One evening while they were eating take-out Chinese food because Lisa had been too tired to cook, Andrew had asked, "What happened to lover-boy?"

Lisa glared at him. "His name is Avery and it's none of your business."

"Avrey!" Abby shouted with a big grin.

Andrew scowled. Lisa figured he didn't appreciate that his daughter liked Avery enough to have learned to say his name. His discomfort made her feel a little better.

As the days, then weeks went by, Lisa grew more and more irritated with Andrew. He seemed to be doing fine getting around on his own while she was at work, but when she was home, he'd ask her to bring him every little thing. He also made messes wherever he went. He left food out in the kitchen which, of course, Bailey helped himself to, and his clothes all over his room that she'd have to pick up. She felt like his cook, his maid, and his nurse. Actually, it wasn't much different than when they'd been married, except he couldn't walk very well. Having him around again reminded her of how bad their marriage had been, and maybe Katrina had done her a favor by taking him away. Now, she wished Katrina had stayed around so he'd be her problem.

When two weeks came and went and Andrew was still living at her house, she became even more frustrated. Especially when he refused to help with anything. On Halloween night, she dressed Abby in her fuzzy puppy costume—she'd wanted to dress up like Bailey—and bundled herself up to go trick or treating with Kristen and Marie. The weather was cold and there was a chance of snow later in the evening, so the women wanted to get the toddlers out early. Lisa had asked Andrew to sit by the door and pass out candy to the children as they came by.

"I don't want to," he whined like a child.

"Oh, come on," she urged him. "You can sit in your wheelchair, hang a camera around your neck, and pretend you're Jimmy Stewart in *Rear Window*. It'll be fun."

"No. I don't want to. It's too cold to sit outside or by the door."

She was so angry with him that she complained to Kristen as they walked from house to house in the crisp night air. "He's being a jerk—just like when we were married. I wish he'd go back to his own place."

"Wasn't he supposed to stay only two weeks?" Kristen asked.

"Yes. That was the deal. But at his last appointment, they said they didn't want to put a walking cast on him for another week or two. And he'll still need his crutches after that, at least for a while. I'm going to go crazy if he stays that long."

"Sorry," Kristen said sympathetically. "Isn't there anywhere else he can go? What happened to that girlfriend of his?"

"I have no idea. All I know is she left."

They had crossed the street and were going house to house when suddenly they were in front of Avery's. Lisa hesitated.

"I'll bring the girls up there if you'd like," Kristen said.

Lisa nodded and waited for them on the sidewalk as they went up to his porch. It was surprising he was handing candy out at all, since he hadn't last year. But last year he'd been a hermit. This year, he was Avery. It tore at her heart that she didn't feel comfortable enough to go up there and see him.

"Avrey!" Abby said excitedly when she came back from his house. He'd given both her and Marie a box of animal cookies, knowing that candy wouldn't work for them.

"You saw Avery," Lisa said, trying to sound excited for her daughter. "That's nice."

As they made their way back across the street, Kristen asked, "Is it really over between you two? Can't you try to talk it out?"

"I'm not sure if we can at this point," Lisa told her sadly. "We were pretty angry with each other, and I think we've waited too long to fix it. I guess it wasn't meant to be."

Kristen gave her a sideways glance. "I think it was meant to be. You two were good for each other. Avery isn't as sociable now as he was when you were together. He's regressing back into a hermit. James and Ryan asked him if he wanted to grab a beer the other night and he declined. He needs you, Lisa. And I think you need him, too."

Lisa missed having Avery in her life, too, but right now, she didn't have the energy to try.

When they returned home, Bailey was out in the front yard, running back and forth as the trick or treaters went by. Lisa's blood boiled.

"What was Bailey doing out in the front yard?" she asked angrily when they went inside. "Someone could have accidentally let him out of the gate."

"He was annoying me," Andrew said from his spot on the sofa, his eyes never leaving the game he was watching on television. "He was barking and running around because of the people outside. So I let him out."

"Don't do it again!" Lisa demanded. "The last thing I need is him running around the neighborhood, lost."

"Well, it wouldn't be the worst thing in the world if he got lost," Andrew grumbled.

Lisa walked over and blocked his view of the screen. "Your daughter loves that dog, so don't do it again. Got it?"

"Fine. Sheesh. You don't have to get all huffy."

It snowed that night, and the next, and by the weekend the neighborhood was covered in a white blanket that was sure to stay. Winter had arrived. Saturday night, after a long day of shoveling the driveway and sidewalk and playing with Abby in the snow, Lisa put the tired little girl to bed and collapsed in a chair in the living room where Andrew was still sprawled out on the sofa, watching television. Lisa reached over, grabbed the remote, and shut it off.

"Hey! I was watching that," Andrew complained.

"We need to talk," she said. She watched as Andrew rolled his eyes, like he'd done when they were married, and it would enrage her. Not anymore, though. She was no longer invested in a relationship with him, so she didn't care what he thought of her.

"You said you'd be here for two weeks. The two weeks are over. I think it's time you go home," Lisa told him.

Andrew pushed himself up to sit higher on the sofa. "I know I said two weeks, but it'll probably be a little longer. They said they'd put a walking cast on at the end of next week, and then it'll be easier for me to get around, even though I'll still need crutches. Just let me stay a few more days, then I'll be gone."

Lisa sighed.

"Hey. It hasn't been that bad, has it?" he asked, giving her one of his flirty grins. He knew he was a handsome man and how to use his looks to get his way. Fortunately, she was immune to him.

"I've fulfilled my end of the bargain, Andrew. I'm tired. You need to go home. You've been getting around just fine here. You'll be fine at your place."

"I don't have a downstairs bedroom at the townhouse. And

the bathroom is too small downstairs to maneuver with crutches. Plus, I wouldn't have any help. It's easier here."

"What happened to Katrina? Why can't she help?" Lisa asked, frustrated.

Andrew sighed and ran his hand through his hair. "She's gone. She left me."

"Why? She wanted you when you were married. Why not now?"

"Because I couldn't afford her spending any longer," Andrew said. "She wanted too much. She always wanted to go out to expensive places to eat, expensive vacations, and she wasn't fond of having Abby over every other weekend. We fought about it all the time. I just couldn't afford to keep her happy."

"But I thought she was helpful with Abby."

"She was, but only because she had to be. If it had been up to her, we would never have had Abby stay over."

Lisa frowned. "I don't get it. Why would you sue me for joint custody when your girlfriend didn't even want Abby around?"

Andrew dropped his eyes. He wouldn't look at her. That's when it hit her. She'd been right all along. It had always been about the money, not Abby.

"You couldn't afford Katrina, so you needed to lower your child support payments to have extra money. Right? You were willing to let us struggle so you could have 'fun' with Katrina."

His eyes darted up. "That's not entirely true. I'm just strapped. You don't realize how expensive everything is. Paying child support on top of buying the townhouse and keeping Katrina happy was stressing me out. It hasn't been easy on me, you know."

Lisa snorted. "On you? What about me? I've had to hold everything together around here. I went from being a wife and mother one day to having to find a job and put Abby in day care the next. Do you realize how much day care costs? We're living on a tight budget. A lot tighter than yours. So don't expect any tears from me, mister."

Andrew dropped his head. "I get that now. And I'm sorry I tried to lower the payments. I told you I wouldn't do that again, and I meant it. I know I was being selfish when I ran off and I should never have petitioned to change custody. I do love Abby. I'd do anything for her. You have to believe me on that."

Lisa thought he did look truly remorseful about his behavior. She didn't exactly feel bad for him, but she sort of understood. "Fine. One more week. But then you have to go home," she told him.

He lifted his head and his eyes lit up. "Thanks, Lisa. I'll keep my end of the bargain. I promise."

She nodded. What she really wanted to say was a snide "whatever," but she kept that to herself.

Chapter Twenty

Avery had spent the past two weeks working on his manuscript. He'd given the couple the happy ending he'd wished he and Lisa had, then he'd sent it to his agent, hoping the publisher would like it. If they didn't, well, tough. He'd find another publisher.

Hopefully.

The entire time he worked, he'd look up and gaze at Lisa's house, wondering how things were going there with Andrew. He saw Lisa and Abby come and go, and Kristen walking over there during the day, most likely checking up on the jerk. On Halloween, he'd hoped that Lisa would bring Abby to his door so he could say something, although he wasn't sure what he'd have said. He'd been disappointed when Kristen brought the little girls up and Lisa had waited on the sidewalk. She must have been really mad at him not to even want to come up to his door.

He'd thought a lot about what they'd said to each other that horrible night, and he'd realized something: he hadn't been angry at Lisa for letting Andrew manipulate her. He'd been angry at Andrew. The guy was a jerk in every sense of the word. He shouldn't have used Abby's custody to blackmail Lisa. In fact, Andrew should never have tried to get his child support payments lowered in the first place. He'd been the one who'd left. He lived in a nice new place with all the amenities while his ex-wife pinched pennies. How dare he not be a man and help support his daughter?

Lisa had been right about Avery, too. He didn't understand what it was like to be responsible for a child. He didn't understand everything she'd done to hold their lives together. But he knew one thing for certain. If he were ever lucky enough to have a daughter like little Abby, he'd do anything to protect and care for her.

The day of the snowstorm, Avery had been out shoveling like everyone else on the block and had seen Lisa out there shoveling her own driveway. He'd wanted so bad to go help her, and to play with her and Abby and Bailey in the snow. But he hadn't. He'd just gone inside and watched them, realizing that if he wasn't careful, he'd turn back into that hermit he'd once been. He didn't want to be that guy again. He wanted to be the happy man he'd been when he was around Lisa and Abby. The man Lisa had helped pull out of his shell to live in the world again. He just didn't know how to be that man without Lisa.

After eating yet another meal alone that evening, he stared at the pizza box he'd had delivered and made a decision. He didn't want to eat alone anymore. He didn't want to do anything alone anymore. He desperately missed Lisa and Abby, and he wanted them back in his life—if they'd have him. He'd walk across the street, knock on her door, and apologize to her, beg her, if necessary, to forgive him. He could tolerate Andrew as long as he had Lisa in his life.

Drawing on all his courage, he slipped on his coat and strode out the door and across the street. The air was crisp, and it stung his face as he made his way to Lisa's door. The living room light was on, and just as he was about to knock on her door, he turned toward the bay window and saw Lisa and Andrew sitting there with serious expressions on their faces. They didn't look like they were arguing; they looked like they were deep in discussion. Once, she smiled at Andrew, and his heart ached. Were they discussing their future together? From his point of view, it looked that way.

Losing his nerve, Avery walked back to his own house, went inside, and closed the door on the past.

* * *

Wednesday afternoon, Lisa came home from work, completely exhausted. *Just two more days,* she told herself. Hopefully, he'd be gone by the weekend. She opened the front door and carried Abby inside. Andrew was lying on the sofa, as usual, with a mess of dirty glasses and plates and an open bag of chips on the table next to him. Lisa sighed. *Just two more days!*

Her day had been long and busy at work and the weather wasn't cooperating either. It had rained, then snowed in the afternoon, turning the roads to skating rinks. The drive home, usually taking fewer than twenty minutes, had taken forty because of the slippery conditions.

Abby hurried past Andrew down the hallway, calling for Bailey. Lisa put Abby's bag in the entryway closet, along with her coat, and slipped off her boots. She ignored Andrew as she headed past him into the kitchen. Opening the fridge, she realized she hadn't taken any meat out of the freezer to thaw for dinner. Lisa let out a long, frustrated sigh. She had no idea what they'd eat.

Abby came into the kitchen, a frown on her sweet face. "No Baywee."

"Bailey has to be around here somewhere, sweetie," Lisa said. She followed Abby down the hallway and looked out into the backyard. There was no sign of Bailey anywhere. Frowning, Lisa walked around the house with Abby in tow, searching each of the downstairs rooms. When they made it back to the living room, she stopped and stared at Andrew, who seemed to be in a television trance.

"Where's Bailey?" she said loudly so he'd hear her.

Andrew glanced up. "I put him out in the front yard earlier. He was being a pain, getting into my food."

"You what?" Lisa hadn't seen Bailey in the front yard when they'd walked up the sidewalk. Bailey would have come running had he been there. "You can't put him out front. He could dig under the fence!"

Andrew shrugged. "I'm sure the ground is too frozen for him to dig." He turned back to his program.

"Abby, stay with your dad," Lisa told the little girl. She slipped on her boots, ran out on the porch, and looked around. Bailey was nowhere to be seen in the front yard. As she scanned the fence, she spotted a hole dug out underneath. "Crap!"

Lisa glanced up at the sky. It was cloudy and the sun would set in less than a half hour. She ran into the house to get her coat so she could search for Bailey. "Watch Abby!" she yelled at Andrew. "And I mean *watch* her! I have to go find Bailey." She threw on her coat and headed outside, calling for the dog. She walked carefully on the slippery sidewalk down to the gate. That was when she saw Bailey. He was running in Avery's yard, heading toward his SUV. Avery had just pulled into his driveway and was lifting something out of the back of it.

"Bailey! Come here right now!" Lisa yelled.

The dog looked in her direction; his ears perked up and his

tail wagged happily. Bailey ran toward her, hitting the slippery street. It was then that Lisa saw the car heading straight for him. "No! Bailey, no! Stop!" she yelled, but it was too late. The car braked into a skid and kept sliding and the next thing Lisa saw was the car's grill crashing into Bailey.

* * *

Avery had just pulled out a bag of groceries from the back of his car when he heard Lisa calling for Bailey. He'd looked up to see Bailey running across the street, and then the car slid and hit him head on. Lisa screamed. He dropped the bag and ran toward the dog, scared to death of what he would find.

"Oh my God!" Lisa cried as he and she met in the center of the street at the same time. "Bailey!"

The young girl driver jumped out of the car. "I tried to stop. I really tried. The car kept sliding. I'm so sorry! He ran out so quickly!"

Avery fell to the ground where Bailey lay, deathly still. Lisa stood over him, her hands over her mouth as tears fell down her cheeks.

"Oh my God! What did I do?" Lisa said hysterically.

Avery laid his head on Bailey's chest, hoping, praying the dog was still alive. Lisa and the driver stared at him, both looking like they were in shock.

"Is he…?" Lisa whispered, unable to say the word "dead."

Avery sat up suddenly. "I hear him breathing. He's still alive." His eyes met Lisa's. "We have to get him to the vet. Now!"

Lisa stood frozen for only a second as his words sunk in, then moved into action. "Let's go."

Avery carefully scooped Bailey up with the help of the young driver who'd hit him. They laid Bailey down in the back seat of his SUV, and Lisa pulled off her coat and placed it over him.

"You sit in the back with Bailey, so he doesn't fall off the seat," Avery said to Lisa. "You'll have to give me the directions to the vet."

She nodded. Just then, Kristen came running across the street. "I saw what happened," she exclaimed, looking as shocked as Lisa. "What can I do to help?"

Lisa asked her to call the vet and tell them they were headed there with an emergency. "And could you get Abby? I don't want her there alone with Andrew."

"It's done. Don't worry about anything. Just get Bailey there safely," Kristen told her.

The girl who'd hit Bailey stood by the car, looking lost. "Should I stay?"

Avery shook his head. "No. You can go. We know it wasn't your fault."

"I'm so sorry," she said again, wiping away tears.

"We know," Avery said gently. He hopped behind the wheel. "Are you all set?" he asked Lisa.

"Yes. Go!"

Avery wished he could have sped all the way to the vet's office, but the roads were slippery and heavy with evening traffic. It was hard for him to keep his emotions in check as he listened to Lisa's tearful voice telling Bailey he was a good dog and she loved him. It felt like forever before they pulled up in front of the small brick building. A woman in scrubs and a man in a white coat both rushed out with a stretcher. Avery assumed they must have received Kristen's call.

"What happened?" the vet asked as he and the technician carefully lifted Bailey onto the stretcher.

"A car hit him. He's still breathing, though," Lisa told him. They took him inside with Lisa and Avery right behind them.

"Wait out here," the tech said. "We'll let you know how he is right after we check him."

Lisa watched Bailey being rolled to the back room. Her face was tear-streaked, and her mascara had smeared. Avery's heart went out to her. She was shivering, so he took off his coat and slipped it over her.

"Come on. Let's sit," he said gently. The place was empty since they'd been closing when Kristen had called them. They found a pair of chairs in the small waiting room and sat, side-by-side.

"I can't lose Bailey," Lisa said softly. "Abby will be heart-broken."

"We aren't going to lose Bailey." Avery spoke in a soothing tone. "He's young and strong. He's going to be fine."

Lisa nodded but didn't look convinced. "I shouldn't have called for him. It was a stupid thing to do. He'd be fine right now if I hadn't called for him."

Avery placed his arm around her shoulders in a comforting gesture. "It wasn't your fault. You didn't see the car coming. It was an accident."

"I'm going to kill Andrew," she said with disdain.

Avery's brows shot up. "Why?"

"He's the one who put Bailey in the front yard. If he hadn't done that, Bailey wouldn't have dug under the fence and run across the street."

"Oh. So, things aren't going well between you and Andrew?" Avery asked, surprised.

She gave him a frown. "No. Why would you think they were? I'm counting down the days until he leaves."

Avery thought about what he'd seen through her front

window on Saturday night. They hadn't been discussing their future together like he'd thought. Relief flooded through him. "I just thought, you know, spending so much time together might remind you of the good old days."

Lisa snorted. "I honestly can't remember any good old days. I do know that the first thing I'm going to do is kick him out of the house. He's been taking advantage of our deal way too long, and now this happened. He's out of there!"

If there was ever a perfect time to tell Lisa he was sorry, now was it. He wasn't going to let the moment pass. "Lisa? I'm sorry about everything I said to you the last time we spoke. You were right. I don't understand how hard it is to pinch every penny, and I've never had anyone in my life I was responsible for. I understand now that you did what you had to do for Abby. I hope you'll forgive me."

Her face softened. "Of course I forgive you. And I'm sorry too. I didn't mean to make it sound like your problems were any less important than mine. I was angry and upset, and scared. I think you're pretty amazing." She gave him a small smile. "You keep saving me. Even when I don't think I need saving, there you are. I don't know what I would have done without you tonight."

"Oh, sweetie. That couldn't be any further from the truth," he said, gazing down into her beautiful blue eyes.

She looked at him quizzically, but then the veterinarian came in and interrupted their conversation. Lisa sprung up, bracing for the news about Bailey.

"Bailey is doing okay," the vet said. "He had a pretty good blow to the head, but he's awake now and the X-ray shows no signs of bleeding or swelling in his brain. He has two broken ribs and his right front leg is broken, but otherwise, he's fine."

Lisa let out a long sigh. "Thank goodness. Can we see him?"

"He's drugged up pretty good right now. I'm going to keep him that way for a while, so he doesn't move around and re-injure those ribs. I'll put a cast on his leg and let him sleep tonight. It would be best if he doesn't see you, because dogs tend to get overly excited when they see their owners."

"Oh." Lisa looked disappointed. "How long will he have to stay?"

"I'd like to keep him a couple of days to make sure he rests quietly, then I'd also like to take one more X-ray of his brain before you bring him home. Just to be on the safe side. I'd say he could probably go home by this weekend, or maybe Monday at the latest."

"Can we visit him tomorrow?" Lisa asked.

"Maybe for a few minutes. I know you're anxious to see him, but rest is what's best for him right now." The vet smiled. "He's a pretty lucky dog. To be hit that way and still be alive is rare. I think he has an angel looking over him."

Avery glanced at Lisa, thinking of Abby. Yes, Bailey had two angels who loved him very much.

Avery drove Lisa back to the neighborhood as she texted Kristen to let her know how Bailey was.

"Kristen says she'll keep Abby overnight since the girls are almost ready for bed. Maybe that's a good thing. I don't think I have the energy to explain to her what happened to Bailey. It'll be easier tomorrow."

Avery asked if she wanted to get something to eat, but she shook her head. "There's one more thing I need to do. It's time I told Andrew to get out."

They were just driving up to her house as she said that. When he stopped the car, Avery touched her gently on the arm. "Do you want me to come inside in case things get ugly?"

"Thanks, but I'll be okay. I need to do this one by myself." She leaned over and kissed his lips lightly, then, looking determined, stepped out of the car and headed up the sidewalk.

Chapter Twenty-One

Lisa walked inside her house, went directly over to Andrew, and said, "I want you out of here!"

Andrew stared at her like she was crazy. "What? What's going on?"

"I'll tell you what's going on," she said, barely able to control her anger. "You almost killed your daughter's dog tonight by being careless and letting him out where he didn't belong. You're lazy and selfish and you've overstayed our deal. I want you out of here by noon tomorrow, no excuses."

"Oh, come on, Lisa. This is ridiculous. It's just a dog. Don't I even deserve top billing over a dog?"

"No, you don't." She walked past him to her bedroom and tossed a few personal things and a change of clothing into a tote bag. When she came out, Andrew was still lying on the sofa as if she hadn't said a thing. "You'd better start calling your friends and get someone to take you and your crap out of here tomorrow morning," she told him.

"Who am I supposed to call?" he asked, sounding like a petulant child.

"I don't care!" she yelled. "Call an Uber. Call a moving company. It's not my problem. Just make sure you're gone tomorrow before I get home or I'm calling the police and having you removed."

Andrew glared at her. "All this over a stupid dog that you didn't even want in the first place," he grumbled.

Lisa grew so enraged she could have smacked him over the head. She walked closer and looked him in the eye. "That dog is your daughter's best friend. That dog has become a part of our family and is more loyal than you ever were. So you'd better never say anything like that to me, or around Abby again." She pointed her finger at him. "And you'd better honor our bargain. I kept up my side. If you try to lower Abby's support payments again, I'm suing you. I have a signed document, by you, stating you won't try again. You'd better live up to that promise."

Andrew stared at her, dumbfounded, but didn't say a word. Lisa walked back outside and slammed the door, then stood there a moment, unsure of where she was going. She had planned on going to Kristen's to spend the night, but as she stood on the porch, her eyes were drawn to Avery's house. Exhausted from her emotional day, she let her legs take her to the only place she wanted to go.

Avery opened the door and looked at her with wide eyes. He'd changed into sweats and looked warm, comfortable, and cuddly. "Hi."

"Hi," she managed, suddenly feeling self-conscious about coming here. This wasn't something she'd normally do, but she'd been drawn here after the stressful day she'd had. She forced herself to continue. "Can I stay here with you tonight? After everything, I don't want to be at my house. I don't want to be alone."

He opened his door wider and moved aside. "Sure. Of course. Come in."

Lisa walked in and glanced around. He had a brown leather sofa and chair in the living room along with a television set sitting inside a large cabinet. Beyond that, the kitchen looked nice and neat, the counters clear of the usual items homes had. The walls were bare and there was nothing personal in the rooms. Unopened boxes were piled in the corner. It looked like he'd just moved in, even though he'd been there over a year.

"Am I interrupting your work?" she asked, peering at the front bedroom where the light was still on.

"No. Actually, I've already sent the book off to my agent and editor. It's in their hands now."

"Congratulations," she said. "What are you working on now?" She nodded toward the office.

"I was working on some notes for another book. Thankfully, the ideas never stop."

She smiled. He looked as nervous as she felt.

"Are you hungry?" he asked. "A little magical elf must have picked up the grocery bags I'd dropped and put everything away in my kitchen. I found the fridge full and the rest on the counter."

"That would be Kristen. Our neighbors are amazing. I don't know what I'd do without them."

"They are a great group of people," he agreed.

She followed him into the kitchen, and he opened the fridge.

"Look. She even added a jar of homemade soup. It looks like vegetables and beef." He pointed to the Ball jar in the fridge. "We could have grilled cheese and soup."

"Now that you mention it, I am hungry. That sounds good."

They worked side-by-side in the kitchen heating up the soup and making the grilled cheese. Avery added tomatoes to his sandwich, and Lisa told him to add some to hers. He pulled a bag of chips out of the cupboard and they sat on stools at the counter and ate, each drinking a beer, too.

"This is delicious," she said after taking a bite of the sandwich. "I don't know why I never thought to use tomatoes before."

"It's my mom's recipe. She used mayo on the bread, which I didn't, but it's good that way too."

They ate and talked about the accident, going over every detail again. She told him what she'd said to Andrew, and that she hoped he'd be gone by tomorrow morning.

"That's why you didn't want to stay there tonight?" he asked.

She nodded but didn't add that she hadn't wanted to be anywhere else but here, with Avery.

"Don't take offense, but it looks like you never really unpacked. Didn't you think you'd live here very long?" she asked.

"I don't know what I was thinking," he said. "I bought this place because it was still close to the trails around Lake Harriet, and because it looked like a quiet neighborhood where I could hide out and write. I was so angry then that I just never took the time to make this a home."

"What about now?" Lisa asked. "Do you want to make it your home now? Or are you still thinking about buying back your other house across from the lake?"

"I don't know," he said honestly. "I did love that house, but I like where I am right now, too." He smiled at her. "I especially like my neighbors."

They cleaned up their mess and loaded the dishwasher, then Lisa went to sit on the sofa and Avery sat down near her. She yawned. She was suddenly so drained from all that had happened that day. Avery moved closer to her and she rested her head on his shoulder.

"What did you mean tonight at the vet's when you said that saving me couldn't be further from the truth?" she asked.

"Oh. That." He slipped his arm around her shoulders and she snuggled in closer to him. "You said I was always saving you. But the truth is, you saved me."

Lisa lifted her head and looked at him curiously. "I saved you?"

"Yes. Sure, I've helped you with some things, but they were all things you could have done yourself. The truth is, you and Abby and even Bailey are the ones who saved me. From myself. From being an angry, hateful, spiteful hermit." He laughed a little and Lisa smiled.

"I'm sure you would have gotten over all that at some point without us," she said.

Avery turned serious. "I'm not sure I would have. My writing was suffering, I wasn't open to meeting anyone new or making friends, and I was just growing more bitter by the day. But after I met you, my life turned around. I could write again, and I could feel other things besides anger." He reached for her hand. "You changed my life. I'm happy again. And when we fought about Andrew, I thought I'd lost you and that happiness. It was the worst thing I'd ever experienced. Worse than my marriage breaking up. Worse than losing my house. Because losing you and Abby was like losing the most precious gift anyone has ever given me."

Tears filled her eyes as she listened to his words. "I felt the same way about losing you. I wanted to call and apologize, but I didn't. I felt like I had way too much going on in my life and I didn't want to complicate yours any more than it already was. But I missed you so much."

"I'm falling in love with you, Lisa," Avery said tenderly. "Is that weird to say? After only knowing each other a few weeks?"

She shook her head and smiled as tears fell down her cheeks.

"No. Because I'm falling for you, too."

He leaned down and their lips met in a soft kiss. She circled her arms around his neck, and he wrapped his around her, too, and soon their kiss deepened. When they finally pulled away, Avery grinned at her.

"What?" she said, smiling back.

"This is all because of a silly black and white dog named Bailey."

"Thank goodness for Bailey," she whispered.

Later, Avery offered to make up the sofa for himself and let her have the bed.

"Do you mind if I sleep with you?" she asked. "I don't want to be alone tonight."

He nodded and when they slipped into bed, he curled his body around hers, holding her tightly. Safe and warm in his embrace, Lisa, for the first time in a long time, felt loved. She knew that she had the strength to face whatever tomorrow would bring because of her love for Avery.

* * *

Lisa called work the next morning to take a personal day. She needed to make sure Andrew had left, check on Bailey, and explain to Abby that her best friend was in the animal hospital and would be home soon.

Avery went with her to pick up Abby and then took them out to breakfast. There, they explained to Abby, in as simple of terms as possible, about what had happened to Bailey.

"Baywee come home?" the little girl asked, looking up at her mom with sad eyes.

"Yes, sweetie. He's coming home in a few days. But we'll

have to take care of him, like we took care of you after you came home from the hospital. Do you remember that?" Lisa said.

"Okay. Baywee get a lot of love," she told her mother.

Lisa smiled and kissed her on the cheek. "Yes. We'll give him a lot of love." She glanced up at Avery. "We owe Bailey a lot."

Avery grinned back and winked.

Avery drove them to the veterinarian's and the three were allowed to go into the kennel and see Bailey. The dog was lying on a blanket, sleeping, but he opened his eyes when he heard them. He didn't move much, only wagged his tail as Lisa and Abby knelt beside him and pet him gently.

"Love Baywee," Abby said, and laid her head on the dog's back.

Tears sprung up in Lisa's eyes as she watched her daughter. It was so sweet to see how much Abby loved Bailey. He was the puppy Lisa hadn't wanted, but now, all she wanted was for Bailey to be home and healthy again.

"Where to now?" Avery asked as they piled back into the car.

Lisa looked at the time on her phone. "Well, I guess we should check to see if he left the house yet." She made a point not to say Andrew's name in front of Abby. After all, he was her father and she didn't want her own opinions of him pressed onto Abby.

Avery drove them home. "Do you want me to go inside with you?"

"We'll be okay. I'll talk to you later," she said. She wanted to kiss him but refrained. That was yet another thing she'd have to slowly let Abby get used to. Luckily, Avery understood.

When she walked in the front door, the house was still a mess, but Andrew wasn't perched on the sofa as he'd been the entire time, and the television was turned off. She headed for the back bedroom and it was empty too. Lisa let out a long sigh. She finally had her life back.

As she began picking up the dishes and empty food bags, and Abby was playing with toys on the floor, she found a note on the kitchen counter. *I'm sorry.* That was all it said, but it was enough. At least Andrew had acknowledged he'd been in the wrong. It didn't absolve him of everything, but at least it was a start.

She looked over at Abby and her heart filled with love for her daughter. Even though she knew she'd forever be tied to Andrew, she could live with it. Because she had Abby: the most important part of her life. She hoped that someday, maybe Avery would be a part of their life together, too.

Chapter Twenty-Two

Avery was excited about Thanksgiving this year. Last year he'd spent the day alone in his house, eating pizza. This year, he'd be with Lisa and Abby, and Kristen, Ryan, and Marie were also joining them. It would be like a good, old-fashioned holiday, and he was thankful to be a part of it.

Avery had a lot to be thankful for. Meeting Lisa and Abby had changed his life. He was happy, something he hadn't experienced for a long time. They filled his heart with love and joy, and he couldn't imagine life without either of them. And then there was Bailey. He considered Bailey his guiding angel, even if he'd once thought of him as the annoying dog across the street. Bailey had come home from the vet's a few days after the accident with a cast on his leg. He'd moved slowly and awkwardly for a time but soon turned back into the busy dog he'd been before he'd been hit. The cast didn't seem to slow him down. He was alive, and that was something Avery was very thankful for.

Avery had also heard from his agent that the publisher had loved his book and wanted to sign him to a new three-book contract. He was back on track again, and the ideas were flowing. Avery was excited about the new book hitting the shelves—in a year—and how his readers would react to it. He'd used his life as the basis for it, so it meant more to him than any book he'd ever written. Most of all, he hoped that Lisa would like it. All of his heart had gone into it because of her.

A light snow was falling that Wednesday afternoon as he stood in his kitchen, cutting up veggies. He'd volunteered to bring the vegetable plate and dip—the only thing he could actually make and not ruin. He knew that Lisa was already home from work, doing all the prep work it took to make such a large dinner. Kristen had volunteered to make the pies—pumpkin and apple. Avery's mouth watered at the thought of tomorrow's dinner. Like a little child at Christmas, he could hardly wait.

As he was finishing up the vegetables and storing them in the refrigerator, his phone rang. He looked at the screen and frowned. Animal Rescue. It had to be a wrong number. Still, he answered it. "Hello."

"Hello?" a woman's voice said on the other end of the line. "Is this Avery McKinnon?"

"Yes."

"I'm Jenna Hall. I work at the Animal Rescue in White Bear Lake."

Avery's interest piqued. "What can I do for you?"

"A dog was brought in on Monday, and today, when the veterinarian was doing a routine check-up on her, he happened to scan her for a chip. Your name came up as the owner. We were a little concerned, considering the person who dropped her off was named Ross Gunderson. Are you missing a dog?"

Avery's heart leapt. "Is she an Irish Setter named Maddie?" he asked, hopefully.

"Well, she's an Irish Setter, but he wrote her name as Red."

"If she's registered under my name, it's Maddie," Avery said, hardly able to contain his excitement. "My ex-wife took the dog and Ross Gunderson is her boyfriend. They must have dropped her off there."

"Oh, I see," the woman said. "Unfortunately, that isn't as uncommon as you'd think. Under the circumstances, we'd be happy to give your dog back if you want her."

"Yes! I want her. I can come right now," he said excitedly. He couldn't believe it. He was getting Maddie back. He didn't even care that Melissa had tried to get rid of Maddie instead of just giving her back to him. It only mattered that he knew where Maddie was, and he could have her.

After hanging up, he grabbed his coat and slipped on his shoes, then hurried across the street to Lisa's house. When she answered the door, he pulled her into a hug.

Lisa laughed. "What's this all about?"

"I'm going to get Maddie back! I have to drive to White Bear Lake. Do you want to come with?"

"You're getting Maddie back? That's wonderful! How did it happen?" Lisa asked.

"I'll explain on the way," he said excitedly."

Lisa called Kristen, who said she'd be happy to watch Abby for a while. After dropping Abby off next door, Avery and Lisa hopped into his car and took highway 35W to White Bear Lake. On a normal day, it would have only been a half-hour drive, but today, at rush hour and with the snow coming down, it was taking much longer.

"I can't believe that Melissa would surrender your dog to a humane society instead of just giving her back to you," Lisa said after Avery had told her what had happened. "That's just cruel."

"That's Melissa," he said. "Cruella De Vil. But I don't even care now. I just want Maddie back."

"Thank goodness they scanned her for a chip."

"Right? Melissa hadn't counted on that. She never took an interest in Maddie, so she didn't know I'd had one put in her. Now, I'm so glad I did."

Finally, they reached the address the woman had given him. It was Jenna's private home, since most of the animals lived in foster homes. He could hardly contain his excitement as they walked up to the door. Lisa smiled up at him and slid her arm through his as they waited for the door to open.

A small woman with straight dark hair pulled back into a ponytail answered. "Hi. Are you Avery?" she asked.

"I am," he said, looking past her for some sign of Maddie.

"Come in. There's someone here who I'm sure would love to see you." She opened the door wider and there, lying in the living room next to a young boy, was a beautiful Irish Setter.

"Maddie?" Avery said, walking inside.

The dog's ears perked up and her eyes grew bright. She was up in a flash and ran into Avery's waiting arms.

Avery knelt and buried his face in Maddie's silky fur. It had been far too long since he'd seen his beloved pet. Tears filled his eyes and he didn't care who saw them. He had his Maddie back, and that was all he cared about in that instant.

Lisa knelt beside him and placed a hand on his back. "Hi, Maddie," she said softly. "I've heard a lot about you, girl."

The dog snuggled the hand she offered and then was back in Avery's arms.

"I guess that's all the convincing I need that this is your dog," Jenny said, smiling warmly at them. "Nothing makes me happier than reuniting a pet with its owner."

Avery wiped his eyes and stood, one hand still on Maddie. "Thank you so much for taking care of her. I'll be happy to pay any fee there is to cover her expenses."

"No fee is necessary," Jenny said. "The person who surrendered her paid a fee to do so, and since Maddie is your dog, and shouldn't have been brought to the shelter to begin with, we won't charge you." She grinned. "But donations are always welcome."

Avery reached in his pocket and pulled out two-hundred dollars. "I'm happy to make a donation," he said. "And I'll keep you on my list of places to donate in the future as well."

Jenny's face brightened. "Thank you. We greatly appreciate it."

She gave Avery the dog's harness and leash so they could take her to the car. "If you decide to press charges against the man who brought Maddie in, please don't hesitate to ask us for documentation. We'll be happy to supply it."

"Thank you," Avery said. "But I doubt that will be necessary. I'm just thankful to have her back."

They walked out to the car and Avery placed Maddie in the backseat and they got in the front. All the way home, Avery kept looking in his rearview mirror at Maddie, unable to believe he finally had her back after a year of worrying about her.

"She's not going anywhere now," Lisa teased him as he stared into the mirror for the hundredth time. "She's yours for good."

"I know," he said, smiling over at her. "I just can't believe it, though. This has made me so happy. It's the best Thanksgiving ever!"

She held his free hand and smiled over at him. "Mine, too," she said. Her words warmed his heart.

Once they were home, Lisa went to get Abby, and Avery brought Maddie into her house to meet Bailey. The two dogs circled each other a couple of times, then they must have decided they liked what they saw because they both laid down by the fireplace and enjoyed the warmth.

"Are they friends?" Lisa asked when she came in carrying Abby.

"It looks like it," Avery said.

"Puppy!" Abby said excitedly.

Avery laughed. Maddie was tall and at least fifty-five pounds, definitely not a puppy, but he found it cute that Abby called her that.

"This is Maddie," he said, taking Abby in his arms and bringing her over to meet his dog. "Look. She has pretty red hair like yours."

"Pretty puppy," Abby said, as Avery set her down by Maddie. He knew she was good with children and felt safe having Abby beside her. Abby reached out and ran her fingers through Maddie's soft fur. She giggled.

"Now you have two dogs to look out for you," Avery said. Abby continued to pet Maddie and also Bailey. She was in puppy heaven.

"She's a lucky little girl," Lisa said, coming to stand beside Avery.

He wrapped an arm around her. "I think we're all lucky." He winked at her and she smiled back. He loved her smile.

The next day everyone gathered at Lisa's house, Sam, Bailey, and Maddie included. The dogs, luckily, all got along well. The smell of turkey cooking in the oven and freshly baked pies was delicious. Avery inhaled deeply. This was a day he never wanted to forget. Moments like this were precious. They were memories that lasted a lifetime, and he wanted to absorb every second.

Before they ate, he took Lisa aside and handed her something.

"What's this?" she asked. When she turned it over in her hand, she saw it was his manuscript, *Saving Jenkins*. Her eyes widened. "Is this your new book?"

"Yes. Fresh off my printer. You get to read a copy long before it's published. I wanted you to have it because you're the one who inspired this story."

"I can't wait to read it." She grinned mischievously at him. "Are you Jenkins?"

"Read the book and find out," he said.

"Does this mean your publisher liked it?" she asked.

"Yes. They loved it. They offered me a three-book contract, which I've taken. I finally don't have to worry about money again. Melissa will never get her hands on these royalties."

"That's wonderful." Lisa wrapped her arms around him and kissed him warmly. Pulling away, her smiled faded. "Does this mean you're going to move back into your former house?"

Avery saw she looked unhappy at the prospect of his moving even a few blocks away. He had thought briefly about it but decided against it. "No. I'm staying put. I love this neighborhood and my neighbors." He pulled her closer. "Especially one neighbor in particular. A pretty blond woman who is sometimes harried and stressed, but always kind and beautiful, who has a sweet little red-headed baby girl and a Border Collie that pulls a Houdini every now and again."

Her smile lit up her face. "I'm glad you're staying. You'll never find someone like that again, anywhere."

He laughed. "No. I hope not. I've found everything I want, right here." He kissed her then, as Kristen and Ryan grinned knowingly from the kitchen, and Abby and Marie giggled, and the dogs ran circles around them.

-END-

About the Author

Deanna Lynn Sletten is the author of MISS ETTA, MAGGIE'S TURN, FINDING LIBBIE, ONE WRONG TURN, and several other titles. She writes heartwarming women's fiction, historical fiction, and romance novels with unforgettable characters. She has also written one middle-grade novel that takes you on the adventure of a lifetime. Deanna believes in fate, destiny, love at first sight, soul mates, second chances, and happily ever after, and her novels reflect that.

Deanna is married and has two grown children. When not writing, she enjoys walking the wooded trails around her home with her beautiful Australian Shepherd, traveling, and relaxing on the lake.

Deanna loves hearing from her readers.

Connect with her at:

Her website: www.deannalsletten.com

Blog: www.deannalynnsletten.com

Facebook: www.facebook.com/deannalynnsletten

Twitter: www.twitter.com/deannalsletten

Printed in Great Britain
by Amazon